DARK RULES

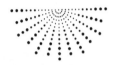

SUMMER COOPER

DARK RULES

SUMMER COOPER

CHAPTER 1

Emily

*H*ad you ever wanted a hole to just open up and swallow you whole? How many times in your life had you thought that? Or read it? Even heard it, maybe? It'd been thought countless times, yet here I was, countless plus one. I had no idea what to do.

I'd had a secret lover, one my family didn't know about. And my lover didn't know who I was. If he knew, his perspective of me would have changed, because I was a Thompson. The only daughter of a man who commanded one of the most powerful, well-known hotel chains in the world.

Now a family-operated business, we had hotels that sprawled not only across America but the globe. We had money, power, and a fleet of cars, boats, and airplanes at our fingertips. I had never wanted for anything, in my entire life. If you didn't count respect and affection.

Which was part of the reason I'd had a secret lover. I didn't want my family to know about him, and now that I knew who he was, I didn't want him to know who I was. I just wanted a nice, uncomplicated relationship. One where I could have as much sex as I wanted to have and then move on, to live out the rest of my life in whatever way it worked out.

This mess, this infernal, laughable mess, wasn't what I'd planned on. I'd put my phone down and stared at the walls until my eyes felt as if they were about to melt. It had been two hours since I'd met with my brother. Two hours in which I was supposed to ponder my future. Have the man of my dreams fuck me into jelly-legged silliness, while I lied to him, or throw it all away and hope my family never found out what I'd done.

I could, of course, always tell him who I really was. He'd seen my face now; if he'd happened to catch me in a picture with my brothers or father, he'd know who I was immediately. I had rarely allowed myself to be photographed, however, so that was a point in my favor. The problem was, I might be known in some of the circles the rather sexy Dylan James wanted to take me into.

We'd discussed new worlds, secret worlds, that he'd wanted to introduce me to. Worlds where powerful men met with even more powerful women, women who could bring a man to his knees, simply by getting on hers in an ultimately pretty pose of submission.

I'd wanted to take part in those worlds, with Dylan, but not if it meant drama that I could really live without. I'd had enough drama in my life with my brothers and their wives. And my father, when he bothered to come back. At first, when I'd told my brothers to find a nanny, I wasn't on duty anymore, they hadn't taken me seriously. Once I changed my phone number, they'd start to realize there was a real problem.

I'd wanted a life. Which brought me back to my original problem. Who should you choose when pleasure, lust, and adventure were in competition with family, hectic travel, bedtime stories, and diapers? I was conscious that I should have chosen my family, but Dylan was a temptation I could not throw away easily. Dylan was all mine, while they just wanted what I could provide them.

I'd remembered his eyes, those seductive gray eyes, and how they looked when he'd finally found his peak. Even now, I felt a twinge of need inside of me. I'd wanted him desperately; that was obvious, if I had to question where my loyalties rested in this whole scenario.

I'd thought about calling Roxie to get her opinion, but she was probably asleep or with Freddie. I couldn't call Jesse, she was my sister in law now, and she wasn't my best friend forever anymore. She belonged to Trent, and that made her off limits to me now. That had hurt a lot when it finally dawned on me, that she wasn't going to be around for me as much anymore. Then they had children, and well, I'd been left alone.

I'd had no other adult friends until I met Roxie, and things changed for me. I started to see how much I'd given up for my family, and what I'd missed in life. They'd all had a chance to be wild, to make stupid decisions, and to make mistakes, the kind that made you smile, even though it shouldn't. I'd never had that chance.

I'd been an adult from the moment I was born. As the baby of the family, I should have been spoiled, and in many ways I was. But then

I'd hit puberty, and somehow, I'd become a nanny for my brothers. That hadn't changed, even when they had their children.

Now, I had Dylan. I didn't feel so alone anymore, even if the time we had together was meant to be short. Two weeks, that was what he'd offered me. Two weeks that would change my life, give me memories to pull out on the loneliest of nights, when I couldn't escape the boredom my life had turned out to be.

With a deep sigh, I'd got up from the couch I'd found myself on and went to the large window in the living room. My view wasn't that great, but I could see that it was getting dark outside. I had to make a decision soon.

Dylan was waiting for me to call.

I knew I couldn't say no to him. We'd only had a short time together, but I knew already that he was what I'd always wanted. Even if I had only allowed the contemplation of what I wanted in the darkest hours of the night. Dylan checked all the boxes perfectly.

My family would have to deal with it, if they'd ever found out. And really, there wasn't a reason why they should find out. If I wore my mask when we were somewhere that I didn't want to be seen, nobody would know it was me. If we went out somewhere more public, where masks weren't acceptable, then I'd have to hope I didn't see anyone who might know my brothers or my family.

It was a risk, but it was necessary to live the fantasy we'd created for each other. We had to be seen in public, the master and his subordinate. I had to be seen to be subservient to him. And he had to be the master, the one who ruled my pleasure.

I'd lost myself in the memories we'd already made and wondered what else he might have in store for me. Gentle moments mixed with rough, that night he began to teach me how to listen to his wishes, the way he'd told me not to come, and I'd obeyed. I didn't know how I'd done it, but I had. I'd waited until he'd allowed me that bliss, and then it was almost too excruciatingly good.

I'd wanted more of that. I'd wanted to be wrung dry, and I knew with those skillful hands of his that Dylan could do it. I'd picked up the contract and signed it with a flourish. I would be his for two more weeks. Then I'd walk away and leave him in the past. I'd go back to my life here at the house I'd rented and find a place for myself in the world.

My family didn't realize it yet, but I was done being the nanny/little sister that did as she was told. I was ready to find a life and spread my wings. If I failed, I had a nest egg many would only dream about falling back on. Financial security wasn't the point, however; the point was that I could live my own life and be a real person.

I loved my nieces and nephews, but that didn't mean I had to be a servant to them. They were children, so they didn't see me that way, but their parents obviously did. Sometimes, in secret moments, I was the most angry at Jesse. She'd been my friend since we were little girls. She'd always had a crush on Trent, but that had ended our friendship.

Then she finally got the man she'd always wanted, and she'd left me behind like an old teddy bear you'd outgrow as you grew up. I would never berate her for it; I couldn't blame her for taking the happiness she now had. I could, secretly, ache to have my friend back.

Something else that was impossible, I reminded myself and went into the kitchen. I took out a bottle of red wine from the fridge and poured a small glass. I sipped at the sweet red and enjoyed the burst of flavors on my tongue.

It reminded me of tasting Dylan's, well, who knew it? I could blush even in the privacy of my own home. I laughed at myself and turned on the music system that played through hidden speakers all over the house. Neil Young's *Harvest Moon* began to play, a song my mother would play for me when I was little, while my father was away on a business trip that never quite ended.

I danced through the house and tried to remember to be happy. I'd just signed my life away to a man who could really hurt me, in more ways than the obvious. I could come off as cold, robotic even sometimes, but that was a defensive mechanism I'd learned a long time ago. If people didn't want to talk to you but were forced to, the coldness you met them with could make the ordeal less burdensome. Get it over with and move on, that had been my motto as a Thompson child.

It had carried me though life well, and it would get me through whatever Dylan had in store for me. Part of the point of our little adventure, though, was that he'd break that wall down that I'd put in place over and over again, until he found the real me. My heart pounded as I thought about it, and anticipation raced through my veins. He would give me everything I'd wanted. Sexually, at least, Dylan would give me total fulfillment.

I'd never have to wonder what *it* felt like again. Sex and completion were things I'd savored now. They were familiar, and I wouldn't have to wonder what sensations made women make *those* faces, those *sounds.* I knew what pleasure felt like, I'd enjoyed a good chocolate cake, and I knew what it felt like to get something that you wanted, but I'd never known what those sensations were from a sexual standpoint.

I'd practiced on myself and learned to control the urges I'd felt since I was a teenager, but I'd never known what it was like to have someone *give* me that kind of sensation. I did now, and I didn't want anything to take that away from me. Especially my family. I'd given them enough of me already, and they didn't get to take this away from me too.

I went back into the living room, checked my new phone, and then went to have a bath. I'd have to be ready for Dylan. He'd told me to take tonight, to think it all through, but I didn't need that time, after all. Not after I'd seen Trent.

I laughed when I remembered the expression on his face when I'd turned to walk away from him earlier. I'd left and come home, even when he'd called after me. He hadn't expected that.

My family seemed to have forgotten something about me. Something I hadn't been able to forget since I was born; I hadn't been allowed to. I was a Thompson. I could be just as arrogant and stubborn as they all were. They walked around so proudly as they silently declared their superior attitudes and inherent right as a Thompson. Well I was now staking claim to that right that belonged to me.

Mainly, I was claiming my right to be left alone, to be left in peace to live my life. If all they wanted was a nanny, then they could go through the process to hire one. I wouldn't be available anymore.

I sank down into my fabulous tub and let the hot water ease the aches from my sore body away. Dylan and I had only just begun to go down the trail that could see my body much more sore than it was now. That was something I actually looked forward to.

It wasn't something I'd ever admit to anyone, except Roxie and Dylan, but I wanted subservience on my terms. I'd longed for unimaginable ways, ways that I hadn't known could be satisfied. But now I knew, and I wasn't about to let anybody stop me. Even if the man who gave me what I craved the most was some kind of economic enemy of my brothers.

We had enough money, and we had loyal clientele. We had a good name in the hotel industry and with our clients. A little competition might be a good thing for them. Instead of declaring Dylan an enemy, Trent should have left the man alone. Dylan was more than capable, he had his own empire on the west coast to prove that.

Trent should have just bowed out and let Dylan get on with his intentions. He should have focused on our empire, not Dylan's. In doing that, he'd lost sight of someone long ignored in the family. Until she was needed, for something that someone else should be doing anyway.

I hated how angry I was with my family; it tore at me, but I couldn't help it. After a lifetime of being the forgotten sister, and then a trusted nanny, I had walked away. It shouldn't have been such a surprise, but obviously I wasn't thought of often enough to make them realize I'd been drowning for a long time and had needed help. I'd found it elsewhere.

In the arms of the enemy. That secret knowledge gave me a thrill. It was a way to pay them back. Sleeping with the enemy, but not for purposes of espionage. Oh no, this wasn't even about revenge. It was about what I'd gain from the experience, how I could get on with my life once this was all done.

No, I was the only one who would win in this little game, even if I was the only one who knew it was being played. I'd go to Dylan, I'd be his, and he'd never even know of the victory he'd been given. But, I would. And that didn't bother me one bit.

CHAPTER 2

Dylan

I heard my phone chirp and saw that I'd had a text from Stephanie. Exchange of our phone numbers had been part of the contract, so that if I wanted her when the club was closed, I could contact her. She was to be at my beck and call. Literally.

I could call her any time I wanted to, and she'd be on her knees in front of me. The possibilities were endless. I could tell her to take me in her mouth and watch her beautiful face as she sucked me to a mind-blowing end, or I could drive inside of her, hard and fast, until we both got off. Or even better, I thought as I sat back on the couch and let the fantasy play, I could bury my face in that sweet spot of hers and fill my senses with the way she tasted, the way she smelled, and the way she felt.

Or I could have all three.

She'd told me she wanted me to be rougher, more in command, and to use a crop on her. I wondered why she'd chosen the crop instead of a whip or a paddle. She'd specifically used the word crop, though. I guessed she'd done some horse riding and had thought about what could be done with that instrument more than once as she rode around.

Or perhaps it was something she'd seen in a movie or something. I knew next to nothing about her, not really. I didn't even know her real name, but I wouldn't push. I didn't give two fucks who knew what I was doing, not really, so I'd used my real name.

She could be reserved, my beautiful little butterfly. Sometimes she would seem distant, as if she was somewhere else, but not often. Stephanie usually focused directly on me, every move I made, when she was with me. It was only in the quiet times, after we'd finished and I didn't want to leave her, that she'd go quiet.

I'd never really wanted to break that silence, because she seemed so lost in those moments. I'd wanted to know things about her, though. What her favorite color was, what kind of music she'd liked, what she liked to eat the most; the little things that all seemed to matter, and that kind of worried me.

I kept reminding myself this was an arrangement, a business transaction, and that I couldn't get involved. That should have alarmed me from the start. I shouldn't have had to remind myself this wasn't a real relationship. It wasn't about long-term plans and honeymoons on the beach, babies in a crib nine months later; this was about sex, dirty, rough, some would even say kinky sex. But sex it was about, and nothing more.

My phone buzzed, and I'd looked down at it. A message from Stephanie. My eyebrow lifted because she wasn't supposed to contact me until tomorrow. Had she changed her mind, was that why she had called me early? My guts twisted into a knot at that thought, and my hand shook as I reached for it to open the screen.

<I'd like to see you tonight.>

Her words made those knots a little tighter. Not much of an explanation.

Then she sent me a picture, a shot of her panties and clothes on the floor. Oh, now that looked far more positive. When she sent me a picture of one of her breasts, covered in bubbles except for her nipple, I knew it was a yes.

<I'm busy, but I'll see if I can fit you in.>

I smirked, I was doing fuck all, but that wasn't the role I had in this game. I was the master, and dismissive was the name of the game at the moment.

<Of course, you're a very important man. I will sit here and wait like a good girl.>

I liked the submission there, the tone that said she would obey.

<That would be wise, princess. Don't touch your pussy, that's mine.>

<No, of course not, sir.>

She didn't offer more, and I knew the game was on. If she'd come right out and demanded sex, I wouldn't be the dominant she'd wanted me to be. By backing off, she'd shown me that she was already playing.

<You must tease your nipples every five minutes, until I tell you to stop.>

<Yes, sir.>

I could just picture her, in the tub, teasing her nipples with soap on her fingers, getting way too hot to stay in the bath. It made me hard, and I fisted my dick through my trousers. I was at home, on my couch, and there wasn't anyone to see me.

I pumped slowly at the shaft for a minute or two, and then I sent her another text.

<Stop, wait five minutes, and then you can do it again. But do not touch your pussy.>

<I won't, sir.>

I knew she probably would, but I'd let it slide if she did. I wanted her primed for me, for when I had her later, and this would make her more than eager.

<Are you touching them now?>

The question would have to be answered, and I knew she'd get frustrated, but she would do it. I smiled a rather smug smirk when it took longer than it should have for her to reply. I watched the screen as she typed, deleted, then started to type again.

<Yes, sir.>

I left her to it for a little while, then I went back to my phone.

<Are you being a good girl for sir?>

She'd been the one to start that, and I'd learned I very much liked it when she did. It was such a sweet form of submission from her; it usually came with a hint of brat hiding just beneath it. Unless I had her pinned down in the throes of wild desire, then it was dirty and carnal when she'd said it.

No reply came, and after five minutes I knew she'd either got out of the tub to come to me, or she'd done the forbidden and touched herself.

I decided to give her a little while longer. I'd put my address in the contract, and she knew I'd expected her to come to my place at some point, so I waited. It wouldn't surprise me in the least if she showed up at my door.

Instead, my phone buzzed.

<I'm sorry, sir, I couldn't help myself.>

It was only a small lesson in control, and she'd been on her own. She admitted what she'd done, though, and that was good.

<I'll let it pass this time, sweetness. Next time, there will be consequences. Do you want to meet me at The Table, for dinner?>

It was an exclusive place, but I knew I could get us a table there. I'd already set it up online by the time she texted me back.

<Of course, sir, what time?>

<I'm leaving now.>

The sun was on its way to bed by the time I arrived at the restaurant and found her in the parking lot. She had on a flirty black pleated skirt that came down to her knees and a white blouse with black buttons that were just the right touch for the place I'd chosen to eat at. "Hello, sweetness."

"Hello, sir." She looked down, demure, apologetic, with a slight blush to her cheeks. My Stephanie.

I gave her a kiss that had her clinging to my black shirt by the time I'd finished with her. When I pulled away, I pushed blonde hair behind her ears and looked into gray eyes a little darker than my own. "You look beautiful."

I bent to her neck as she murmured a reply and licked her just below her jaw. A slight flick of the tongue, just to gather her scent. "But you taste better."

She blinked at me, astonished at my rather public display, but she didn't protest. I took her hand, and we swept into the restaurant with a slight breeze behind us. A breeze that promised much cooler days ahead.

"It's good to see you. Did you bring the contract?" I'd asked offhand. I wasn't worried about it too much right now. I just wanted to know she'd signed it.

"I forgot and left it on my kitchen table."

She'd folded her hands in her lap and dropped her gaze.

"I'll get it next time." I brushed the forgotten document aside. "You signed it; that's all that matters."

"Of course, sir." Which wasn't exactly an admission, but she was here, so she must have signed the contract.

"Excuse me, sir, here is your meal. And yours, madam." The waiter came in to deliver a grilled salmon steak for me, and grilled chicken for Stephanie.

We were silent as we ate. I noted her table manners seemed to be very European, especially the way she ate from the back of her fork, instead of scooping it the way most Americans did. It was a pretty display, but one I'd found unnecessary. It was much easier to scoop your food onto the fork, as intended, but let it go. It was something she'd obviously been taught to do, so who was I to judge.

"How is your dinner?" I'd asked after I'd wiped my mouth and put my silverware down.

"It's really quite nice, sir, thank you." She looked up, her lips slightly parted in a smile, and her eyes glittered with delight.

It wasn't the food that delighted her, however. It was the fact that she'd called me sir; she'd even stressed the word when she'd said it. That was what made those beautiful eyes glitter.

It was slightly dark in here, and we were in a very dark corner, away from the central dining area, where everyone sat who wanted to be seen. I didn't want to expose her too much and had asked for a private table. She sat across from me, in her chair, perfectly respectable and demure. I'd wanted to fuck her against the wall until she screamed out my name, and her mouth made dirty little sounds that would shock the patrons of such a place.

"You may call me Dylan, you know? It is my name." I smiled as she went back to her food.

"I know." She'd popped a cherry tomato in her mouth and chewed before finishing her thought. "I like to call you sir, though. It's rather delicious."

"It is." My little sub could be a vixen when she wanted to be, and obviously she wanted to be now.

"Have you ever swam naked, Stephanie?" If I had to guess, I'd say she never had. But then again, she was full of surprises. Perhaps her family owned some house in the country, some palace with a lake that she'd escape to on hot summer nights.

She looked at me, surprised, and gave a brief smile, before she turned her head away as if admitting the truth embarrassed her.

"It's on my bucket list, but I haven't scratched it off yet." Her eyes came back to mine, and the smile faded away. "Why do you ask?"

"Because I have a heated swimming pool at my place, and I can't stop picturing you swimming in it. Nude and with that hair of yours fanned out behind you."

"Ah," she said with a slight tilt of acknowledgement. "I guess we'll be swimming tonight then."

"Yes, tell me more about this bucket list of yours."

"It's not much really. Little things I'd like to explore or do. I'd like to go to Iceland, just once. We don't have a...," I looked up, surprised that she'd stopped. What had caused that; what had she almost revealed. She wiped it all away with a gleaming smile and carried on. "It's not somewhere I've ever had the chance to go to."

"I see. It's a lovely country, one I wouldn't

mind seeing again." I'd gone as a teenager, to explore the glaciers and do some climbing. I hadn't forgotten that almost slip though. She'd said 'we'. Who was this we, her family perhaps?

"I'd also like to see the remains of Pompeii and explore the shipwrecks beneath the water in Greece."

"Oh?" A history buff then, very good. "And what else? Anything naughtier on that list?'

"You've added a few things and ticked off a few." She gave me that vixen's smile all over again, and I wanted to get her home. Wipe that smile off of her face and replace it with an expression of pure ecstasy.

"Do you want anything else? Another glass of wine, perhaps?" I offered the delay smoothly, as if I wasn't screaming internally that I just wanted to get her home.

"No, I think I'm finished with food for the night." There was something different about her, something that wasn't necessarily aloof, but *was* setting off alarm bells. It was almost as if she had taken this new contract on as a challenge, and where I'd had a perfectly submissive mistress within my grasp, I now had a seductress, bent on winning some kind of game.

Her eyes fell to the table, to the glass of wine between her fingers. No, perhaps aloof wasn't right. Maybe she was using bravado, seduction, in an odd way, to keep me at arm's length.

That was an odd thought, but it might be true. Had something happened in the few hours since I'd seen her last? I had to wonder, but she soon distracted me and asked if we could go now. She suggested she wanted to see my home, and I was more than willing to show it to her.

I'd paid for our meal and we headed out, Stephanie in the protective arm I kept around her to hide who she was, though it wasn't so obvious that was what I'd done. I led her out to her car, and when she had buckled up and pulled out of her parking spot, I pulled out to allow her to follow me home.

The drive home gave me time to think and go over the evening so far. Something was on Stephanie's mind, but she wasn't talking about it. That was fine with me; I wasn't after a relationship after all, just a good time for a couple of weeks. Or so I kept reminding myself. It didn't take long to get back to my place, it was an apartment, but I had an indoor, heated pool in that space. Money could buy you almost anything you'd want, and I'd wanted a heated pool.

Swimming was one of the ways I'd kept fit, and I didn't see a need to swim in cold water. Especially when you added Stephanie to that water. Although, with her in the pool, I might not have needed heated water to keep me warm.

CHAPTER 3

Emily

Dylan called his place an apartment. What he didn't say was that this 'apartment' was a penthouse at the very top of one of the buildings in the city. It overlooked the ocean on one side and had an excellent view of the lights and attractions below. The entire place, decorated in a cold, masculine taste, very minimalist, with black furniture and glass tables, wasn't inviting if you were a woman looking to create a lasting relationship with a family in the future.

But if you were looking for a man to fuck you into the middle of next week and make you beg for more, well then, Mr. Dylan James was your man. The apartment was indicative of a man who liked his control, who tended to his needs, but wasn't the kind to put up with unnecessary fluff. In essence, his 'apartment' told me just what I'd already known about him.

"Would you like another drink?" he'd asked as we walked through the place. A small living room with a long couch, one black leather chair, a glass table, and a television went by, and white painted walls were a blur uninterrupted by portraits of any kind. The floors were some kind of black wood, and I glanced around to see a bathroom, a bedroom with a red duvet, another empty room, or at least it looked empty with the door only partially opened, and then the kitchen.

"There's a study through there"—he pointed off to the left—"and through there is the pool and gym area."

I could see a door to the right and wondered what delights waited for me in that room.

"Could I have some water, please?" I asked, when he went to the sink in the island in the middle of the kitchen.

"Of course, I'm sorry." He went to the fridge and pulled out a bottle of water. The same brand from the club. I'd said it was the kind I preferred, and he'd remembered.

I felt a smile pull at my lips as I took the bottle and opened it. After a few sips, I put the bottle down and walked over to him. "Now, sir, when do we begin?"

I let my lips part, and my eyes went down as I sank to my knees. There'd been nothing about how a sub should act in this contract, only that I was to be the sub. I liked this moment of our time together, though, and loved the way he looked at me when I did it. As if he was on top of the world. As if I'd given him that world and wanted to put it all right back at my feet.

His hand came down, a finger stroked my cheek as I looked up at him, my heart in my throat. He was my family's enemy and should be off limits to me. Something about that gave this moment a dark edge that I couldn't turn away from. It heightened my excitement, that I might be caught, that they might learn about my betrayal. That he might.

That part didn't sit so well with me. As far as I knew, Dylan hadn't done anything to earn Trent's enmity; he'd only wanted to make his way into the hotel industry on this side of the country. It was Trent's childishness that made Dylan forbidden fruit. If he found out what I'd done, then he would have to deal with it. I hadn't really betrayed anything, not really.

Or so I explained it to myself as desire began to flood through me. Dylan took my hair in his hand, bunched it within his fist, and pulled my head back. Not so tight that it hurt, but enough to know he had my hair firmly in his grip. "And what do you want tonight, Stephanie?"

"Whatever you desire, sir. That's all I ask for." The words were out of my mouth without a second thought. He could have whatever he wanted of me. My gaze dropped to the place before me, the zipper of his pants. It was bulging now, and I knew my pose, my submission, had done that to him.

"That's not what I asked, pet. I asked you what you wanted." His tone was stronger, more forceful, but I couldn't hear him because all I heard was the sound of his zipper as it moved down. His hand had covered the panels of his trousers, and now his thumb moved into his pants to hook his cock as he brought it out of the darkness.

He didn't have on briefs, just his trousers, and I knew that was in anticipation of our meeting. He held himself in his hand, out to me, and my head moved closer, my mouth opened, ready for the invasion. I felt my lips against the head and my mouth opened, hungry to take him in, but he tugged at my hair still wrapped around his hand. "Ah, ah, pet. I asked you what you wanted."

I glanced up, my hands on the floor, as irritation surged through me. "I want to taste you."

"Then you should ask, pet. You can't just take, now can you?" His smirk made me want to scratch him, but at the same time, it made me want to dig my nails into the firm muscles of his ass and pull him deeper into my face.

"No, sir. You're right. I'm sorry." I ducked my head, dutifully, and waited. He didn't say anything, so I looked up after a long moment.

"Well?" He still had that one hand on his cock, and I wanted it so much. I wanted to feel the way it popped into my mouth once the head was in, the way he slid over my tongue so smoothly.

"I want to suck you, sir." I bit my lip and hoped my statement pleased him.

"Ah, but that's a demand. Not a request." He stroked himself, and all the soft places inside of me melted with yearning. I wanted to do that, with my hand and my mouth. But he'd decided to tease me, to make me ask for exactly what I wanted from him.

"I see." I nudged my knees apart just a fraction, so that the edge of my skirt moved and the space between my knees was on view. Not a lot, not vulgarly, but enough to catch his eyes, if he looked. "May I suck your cock, sir?"

His lips parted on an inhaled breath, and his eyes turned even hotter than they had been. A thrill of delight surged through me at the evidence of his desire, his appreciation of my submission given properly, at last. "Of course, you may, my darling."

I reached for him, took him in my small hand, still amazed at how he filled it. How could that possibly fit inside of me, I wondered, but then, I opened my lips, leaned in, and felt him slide in, slick silk against my soft lips. My jaw opened wide, and he went further, deeper into my mouth. I stopped and inhaled, my hands to each side of his cock now, the fingers of my right hand grasped around him. I only had half of him in my mouth, and I already felt full.

I closed my lips around him, savored his taste, inhaled around him, and sucked my way up his length. I felt his fingers tug at my hair as they clenched on top of my head. He rocked on his feet as I began to move down on him again to push himself deeper into my throat. I liked the sound he made, a growl that he tried to cut off, to hide from me, as I sucked at him all over again.

I moved faster and took him deeper, until he lost his control and growled above me. I was, by no means, an expert at any of this, but I could follow the cues he gave me. His fingers clenched tightly in my hair, until I thought he might have pulled a few stands from my head. I didn't care and felt the tug of pain as pleasure. I inhaled through my nose, desperate for a sound, a move, that would tell me I'd driven him deeper.

I'd wanted to please him, he was the man I'd chosen to serve, and I wanted to make him crave me. I wanted him to crave my touch as much as I craved his. It wasn't something I'd have admitted just then, but it was something I began to understand. Two days hadn't been enough; two weeks might not be enough either. He had so much to teach me, so much to make me feel, and I wanted it all.

I felt a slickness between my thighs from my own excitement. I could feel a throb from my clit, a throb that was need and pleasure combined. Soon enough, he'd touch me or he'd tease me, and I didn't care which it was he chose.

I was his to do with as he pleased, to an extent, but I hadn't started this game to be a wimp and tap out at the first sign of danger. I wanted that edge of I can't take anymore and pure bliss. He'd given me a taste of it already, and I'd wanted more.

I hummed happily against him as he moved to the back of my mouth, near my throat, and Dylan gasped again. I grabbed at his ass and dug my nails in to hang on as he rocked into my face, into my throat, deeper and deeper with each thrust. I moaned around him, lost in the moment, lost in his arousal, in my own. My nipples tightened when he groaned again, and need flared even hotter in my abdomen, but right now, all I could do was hang on.

My sir needed to come, and I was going to make sure he did. It was my duty, after all.

I sucked, I flicked my tongue, and I dug my nails deeper into his flesh, until he strangled out another growl, and his cock pulsed in my mouth. He was over the edge, and I took every drop of his pleasure and swallowed it gladly. My time would come, and now that the no penetration clause was gone, I knew I had much more to look forward to than a blow job in his kitchen.

Now that we were also in an environment where we could really relax, things could progress even more. The intrigue wasn't quite gone yet, I still hadn't given him the contract, and he still didn't know my real name. I didn't plan on giving up either until I had to. I had signed the contract, but I'd rather not have one at all. Not now that I knew who he was.

I wanted to be his of my own free will, for however long he'd take me.

I wiped at my mouth as he pulled away and sat back. Other than the fact that I was on my knees, and he was doing up his pants, an onlooker wouldn't be able to tell he'd just fucked my face thoroughly. Well, other than my mussed hair, I thought with a smile. I combed through it with my fingers, and he gave me his hand.

"Stand up, Stephanie. Let me look at you." I stood up and looked up to him. He stood a head above me, at least, and his height made me feel small. But I also felt safe, protected, with him near me. As if the world could never reach me, so long as Dylan James was there to keep it at bay.

"Do you like what you see, sir?" I asked, my eyes now down at my toes. I felt his hand under my chin and lifted my eyes up to his.

I might be a full-grown woman, independent and able to take care of herself, but in that moment, I was an eighteen-year-old girl all over again. Uncertainty filled me, and my doubts crept in. I knew he liked me, that he liked our sex play, but would I please him in all ways? Did he want my hair longer or shorter, a different color maybe?

"You're just right. Perfect, pet." A finger brushed my hair behind my right ear, and I licked my lips to wet them before I spoke again.

"Thank you, sir. I'm glad I please you." I swayed toward him, my body still on fire for him. His finger wound around to my cheek, and I leaned in deeper, until our lips were only a breath apart.

"You always please me, Stephanie." His lips brushed against mine, and I wanted to cringe when he said that name. I wanted to tell him it wasn't my name. But would he understand? Would he use me in this stupid war my brother seemed to have started with him.

"My…," I paused, the truth on the tip of my tongue, but I couldn't say it. "My joy knows no bounds, sir."

I moved that fraction of an inch closer and

pressed my lips against his. "Don't you want me, sir?"

"I do, pet, but I'm not in a rush. Are you?" He pulled away, but kept my hand in his.

Something told me he wanted my admission, the honest truth, and not a game, so I pulled air into my lungs and looked up at him with eyes full of hunger. "I ache for you."

Deeper down the hole I fell. Every time I was with this man, I went a little further down the rabbit hole. Soon, I'd find a chess board made of human players and a Mad Hatter; I just knew it. His cocky smile told me I'd been right, he wanted to know all of it and more. Perhaps I'd met the Cheshire Cat, and I just didn't know it yet.

"You'll have all of me, in time. Don't rush life, Stephanie. Sometimes, the best things in life are worth waiting for. Besides, I make the decisions now."

That grin on his face took on a harsh edge that should have made me tremble in fear, but instead, I felt blood rush around in my veins with glee. I'd signed up to be his slave, I'd asked for pain, and he'd taught me a few things about pain already. He'd taught me about the pain of wanting something you couldn't have, that kind that was almost worse than the sting of a switch against your legs. The kind he'd given me so far had grown, blossomed, into an ache that throbbed through me, until I thought I'd go mad. Then he'd given me a little more.

"Remove your clothes for me, pet." We'd made it to the pool room by now, and I saw the large rectangle-shaped structure was lit by underwater lights that turned the water an inviting light green. And beside one edge was a black man and a riding crop.

CHAPTER 4

Emily

*D*ylan moved up behind me, and his hands moved around me to pluck the buttons from the holes on my shirt. "Do you want it, Stephanie?"

He spoke the words casually, as if he hadn't just asked me if I wanted to take a step further into the world he wanted to open for me. I felt my stomach bottom out and put my hand over it. The skin was bare now, and I'd realized he'd pulled my shirt away. I looked down to see the white silk bra and my skirt.

That soon fluttered down my legs to pool at my feet.

"Stephanie?" He paused behind me. His hand on the closure of my bra.

"Yes, sir. I want whatever you have to offer me." I stared at the pool of water as the material around me went slack and disappeared. The air was warm in the room, but I felt my nipples go tight as excitement flooded my veins.

"Good. I may not use it tonight, but do keep in mind that it's there. For you." His fingers dipped into my panties as he spoke behind my ear.

I gasped when his fingers brushed over me, but he didn't go further; he only pushed the material down, until it too was a pool of silky cloth at my feet.

"Get in the water. Let me watch you move." He gave me a gentle nudge, and I took a step toward the pool. The water was warm, as he promised. By the time it was at my breasts I dove in and did a lap around the bottom.

I'd never swam naked, and I found it shockingly nice just how good it felt to slice through the water without impediment. I kicked beneath the water, sex forgotten for a moment as I enjoyed the pure pleasure of being nude in a pool. I was smiling when I broke the surface and swiped my hair back and blinked water from my eyes. "It's nice."

"It is. It's not very often one gets the opportunity to swim naked, much less in a heated pool." He'd removed his shirt, shoes, and unbuttoned his trousers. I saw his socks beside his shoes and smiled. Had he been about to join me?

"I learned to swim in a pool that could have been filled by the waters surrounding Iceland; it was so cold. But I became proficient at it."

"I'm glad you know how to swim." His head tilted as he pushed the zipper down on his trousers. "It looks like you can hold your breath for a while too?"

"Oh, quite a while, sir." Just like that, the tension was returned to the air, and I waited for him to drop the pants with my breath held. I knew what he hid beneath the black slacks, but it was still new to me, still a thrill.

My lips pursed and my eyebrow quirked as I waited in the water for him. Finally, he let the pants go and walked into the warm water to join me. I held my hand out to him, my eyes down once again, and he pulled me to the deep end with him.

Although, I had a feeling I'd been in the deep end from the moment I met Dylan James. He'd pulled me to him, and my legs wrapped around his waist as our chests came together. His lips slid along my jawline and up over my cheek, until he reached my ear.

"I want to be inside of you." A few simple words, but they meant far more than that. He wanted to be in me, yes, but he wanted to be in my head too. "I want to own every single part of you, Stephanie."

I looked up at him, my left hand cupped against the back of his head, and pulled him down to kiss me. I didn't know if I could let him in that deep, I didn't know if I could let anyone that deep. Even Dylan, and he'd seen more of the real me than anyone else ever had.

Instead of words, I gave him action. I kissed him, my tongue a slick slide along the seam of his lips until he opened to let me in. I explored him, slow and easy, the water a warm cocoon around us. His hands gripped at my bottom until his fingers dug into my flesh to press me tighter to him. I felt him nudging at me, a soft but insistent touch that made me wonder. What if I just moved, only a little bit. My virginity would be gone, and he'd have me, totally.

Or, as much as I'd let him have me. It was an odd time to realize that there were aspects I'd continue to hide, parts of myself that I'd never let anyone into, but what could I do? I could only feel, be touched, and wait for what he gave me. I heard a soft sound, deep in his throat, and knew it was appreciation; he'd liked the unsophisticated technique of mine, I'd guessed, but I was learning.

By now, I knew he liked to suck my tongue, that he liked to feel me moan inside of his mouth. I drove my fingers into his hair, held his face to mine as desperation began to drill insistently through my brain. And then, something changed.

I'd noticed a hint of danger to Dylan before, as if there was a side to him I hadn't experienced yet, and for a moment, as he gripped my hand and pulled it behind him, I caught a glimpse of it. A thrill went through me.

At last.

I'd waited for the real moment he finally took control, and just as I'd decided that he'd never really own me, he'd shown a real crack in the persona he'd shown me. I had to think there was a reason Trent hated him and thought he'd killed his real parents; it couldn't just be jealousy, and for the first time, I wondered just how dangerous Dylan actually was.

He had a tight grip on my hand, and he held it

behind him while he walked us to the wall of the pool.

"I really wish you'd brought that signed contract with you, pet." I could see flecks of black in the gray of his eyes as I stared up at him; our eyes locked as I tried to remember to breathe.

"Is it really that important, sir?" My voice shook, but it wasn't fear; it was uncontrolled excitement. I'd broken the rules, and something told me I was about to be punished.

"It's everything, Stephanie." His words were a whisper against my neck, and a shiver ran down my spine when I felt his lips graze the skin below my ear. "You see, I had plans for tonight. I was going to finally find out what it felt like to be inside of you."

His lips closed on a patch of skin and everything that hadn't been tight before suddenly puckered as his teeth grazed me just as he began to suck at me. My hands went to his head, clamped in the brown silk that covered it, and clenched as he tugged a little harder. He'd leave a mark, but I didn't care.

I kind of liked the idea of being marked by him. A sound escaped my throat, and I pressed every inch of my body into his as I tried to remember what we had been talking about. Something about the contract. Maybe, I couldn't remember, not when he groaned loudly, and his hand dived down to find me wet and ready for him. A slick of his finger between my folds, and then he found the part of me that ached the most.

He let go of my skin, but my concentration was on the action of his fingers, not his mouth.

"You want me so much, Stephanie. Your body gives you away. From the way your eyes dilate when I speak to you, to the way your skin tightens when I touch you. And this." He paused to cup me in his hand for just a moment before his fingers went back to their play. "This absolutely *drips* for my dick."

I shook my head eagerly, in total agreement with him. Maybe he wouldn't punish me; maybe he'd finally give us what we both wanted so very much. A sound came from my throat, but it wasn't really a word. I'd meant to say please, but I couldn't make it come out as a word. I'd wanted him too much, and my throat was closed with anticipation.

"So I'm a little confused." His finger on my clit paused, and I wanted to beg him to do it some more, but I knew he wouldn't, not if I asked.

He pulled his hand from between my legs and grasped my right arm to move it up to the wall. It was only then that I saw a clamp. I hadn't noticed it before, and now I could see it could be anything, some kind of clamp for pool equipment, but I knew it wasn't. Something went tight in my lower abdomen, and my heart raced.

I really was about to see the real Dylan, and I felt just the slightest tingle as I realized this could be dangerous. That feeling only heightened when he put my other arm in the clamp, closed the clasp with a *snick*, and did the same to the other. He'd given me a moment to protest, to safe word out of this situation, but I'd let it pass. I looked up at his face and could almost feel the way my eyes dilated.

"You see…" He dropped to his knees then, and my eyes went wide. Why was he on his knees? Wasn't he supposed to be up here with me; wasn't I supposed to be the one down there? He placed his head against my right hip and looked up at me. "I wanted this. This sweet bit of heaven that you carry with you."

I could only swallow at that point and tried to

remember to breathe. I still hadn't quite remembered how to go about that yet. A stray drop of water slid out of my wet hair and down my spine. I shivered as it slid to the middle of my back, but I wasn't sure the shiver came from that.

I thought it was his words, the way he looked up at me with so much naked hunger that I wanted to stroke his face. But my wrists were in the clamps, and I couldn't touch him. Lesson one, a lesson I'd already learned but forgot, had started all over again. He'd taught me this torture before; how could I have forgotten that?

"It's a shame really, Stephanie. I had such plans for this virginal pussy of yours. I was going to fuck this slit into a heaven that opened only for me." His breath against my skin was a new torture, because I wanted it on me there, in that place he now spoke of worshipping. That place where I throbbed for his touch. I could feel the way my hips squirmed against his face. If I moved in just the right way…

"Sir…" I finally said when he didn't move a muscle. I wanted to be free, to move my hips, and I tried to move my hands just a little. The urge to comfort him made me try, but they would not budge from the clamps.

He didn't answer, not at first. Instead, he put his hands on each side of me and opened me up. He blew a breath over the hot, slick skin before he took my clit into his mouth. I groaned then, loudly and without shame. The sensation of his wet mouth and tongue on me set off little sparks of pleasure that just weren't enough. I needed more. He pulled away when my hips began to follow the suction of his mouth, when I began to plead with him for more.

"No, Stephanie, you didn't sign the contract. And that's such a shame." The fingers of his right hand played over me as he spoke, and I looked down to see if he meant it. To see if there was some sign that he might budge.

I'd hoped that he'd just ignore it all and let me have my way, but he'd been serious. Maybe, for now, his resolve was high, I decided, but later, he'd give in. Surely? I didn't want to give him that contract. It seemed silly to me now, and I didn't want to give in to the challenge he'd set.

I'd decided that was probably the gist of my whole problem. He'd insisted on it. I wanted to be a brat, I wanted to challenge him, to make him make me obey. He'd been too gentle so far, and while part of me appreciated that, there was also part of me that felt as if we hadn't taken this far enough yet. As if he hadn't taken enough control.

This was the moment when I'd find out if he was serious about being the dominant person I wanted him to be. I could feel the challenge burning in my eyes, and I knew he'd seen it when he gave a rather smug smile.

"I see." Dylan nodded and sat back on his bottom, palms up on the floor to prop himself up. "What am I to do with you, brat?"

I gave him what I felt was a rather smug smile and spoke. "Whatever you please, sir."

"Ah, but we agreed on there being a contract, Stephanie. That is vital for any of this to happen. How do I know you are truly consenting otherwise? Especially now that I have you in those clamps." His finger pointed in the direction of my wrists, and I squirmed. Surely he wasn't about to end the night just because I hadn't brought the contract.

CHAPTER 5

Dylan

She looked down at me with round eyes that challenged, but also, with eyes that begged. In that moment she was the perfect sub. If only she'd signed that contract, I'd be inside of her now.

I wanted her to feel pain, but the kind of pain that would make her remember to bring that fucking contract next time. I'd wanted her to know that she'd done something wrong, and the consequences of her actions. But I wanted the pain, the consequence, to be worth the defiance, because I could see now, she hadn't forgotten the contract. She'd done this on purpose. To test the boundaries.

I'd dismissed it earlier, desperate to have her, but she'd eased that desperation in the kitchen. If she hadn't gone down on her knees to get me off at the moment, I might have broken, I might have given her what we both wanted, but she'd left the contract at home. Now, we both had to pay.

I spread my legs out in front of me and waited until her gaze had stopped dancing over my body. She looked delicious, inviting, clamped to the wall. Her womanly body was on display there, her thighs an inch or two apart, her breasts high and round. Her nipples were dark with the flush of blood that made them tight. Her skin was pale, except the places where blood turned her skin red as it ran hotly through her veins. Her cheeks were pink, her lips parted, and those incredible eyes were wide open.

I could see she breathed quickly; her excitement given away with the subtle clues she didn't even know she gave me. Her eyes moved again, flicked down to my dick, and went wide. I was hard, ready for her, but she'd decided to deny us that pleasure. A flick and our eyes met. I gave her an evil grin, one that said, 'fuck you, Stephanie', and took my dick in my hand.

"If you won't play by the rules, my dear, I'll just have to play by myself." I said the words softly, but she flinched as if I'd shouted at her. That only made my smile broader.

With my thumb at just the right place, I started to stroke myself and watched. She'd shifted against the wall, her lips so temptingly pink opened up, and her gaze went down. She pulled her lip in between her teeth, and I knew she saw the error of her ways.

I'd brought her to arousal, I'd had her on the path to completion, but then I pulled away. It was similar to what she'd done to me. She'd promised a signed contract, but she hadn't brought it to me. I had to drive that home to her. She must do as I say.

Otherwise, this was a relationship, and I simply didn't do those. I wasn't going to be around town long enough for one thing, and for another, I liked my freedom too much. I didn't want a woman to lay claim to me. I didn't want anybody to have a claim to me. Not even my adoptive parents. I owed them some loyalty, they gave me my life back, after all, but otherwise? No, I was a free agent, and I planned to keep it that way.

"You really fucked up, Stephanie. You really, fuck..." Her legs moved, gave me a show of that pink silk between her thighs, and I had to fight back a groan. I'd wanted to be inside of her so much. I had to stop my hand, had to stop the languid movements over my flesh, before I could speak again. "You really fucked up, pet."

"Sir...," she started to speak, but with a lifted eyebrow, I stopped her.

"No, pet. You had one task. Bring me a signed contract. You didn't bring me that." I felt as if I held the control and moved my hand again. Her eyes went down when she caught the movement, and I saw regret. Good.

I didn't offer her mercy of any kind, because this was a new phase of our relationship. She was about to see a little bit of the me I kept hidden away from the world. The me who needed her to give me everything that was her. I didn't want her possessions, I didn't want her to promise me the world; I wanted her to give me herself.

I knew this was the first challenge she'd set for us both, it was in her nature, but it was my job to answer each of those challenges correctly. To give in to her, to fuck her until we were satiated wasn't good enough. I'd lose face as her dominant, and I wasn't about to do that.

I could handle a sub/dominate relationship that had a set expiration date. That was a contract, an entirely different kind of relationship. If I didn't get my fill in that time, oh well. The contract was over. If she'd want more, but I'd want to walk away, it would be fine. The contract was finished, and so were we.

Good thing I was fine with taking care of myself. Of course, the fact that she was naked and helpless in front of me, my own goddess to worship, certainly helped. I wanted her, but that would have to wait. Until she gave in.

"When you bring me a contract, I will take you, Stephanie. I will tear away what's left of your virginity after a lifetime of activity and I will fuck you until you can't stand up without your legs shaking. I will fuck you while you lie on your back like a wanton, and I will fuck you on your hands and knees as you beg me to go deeper." I had to pause again, the images my words created in my mind were too vivid. I could see her perfectly, that lovely ass on display just for me.

My hand was clamped around my dick, the way the metal clamped around her wrists, and I looked more closely at the place where her hands were. It wasn't too tight, but the image was seductive. Stephanie moved her hand, and the metal pinch into her skin. My eyes narrowed as I focused on that, the way her skin pushed in, soft against the hard, unforgiving edge of the metal clamp. It was a good thing I'd asked the maker to sand down the sharp edges, or she would have bled from that spot.

I hadn't had anyone in those clamps yet, the place was still new, but I'd had those installed the day after I'd met Stephanie. There'd be time for other women later. Once I'd had my fill of her. For now, all I wanted was to have her, to fuck her out of my system, and then I'd think about moving on.

I watched her as she stood there, pinned to my wall. I began to stroke myself again. I looked at her breasts, the way the firm flesh shifted as she began to struggle, for only a moment, before she settled down again. The sway of her hips as she repositioned herself, accepting now of the fact that she would not be free until I told her she was.

When I heard her sigh in resignation, I gave her my eyes again. I let her see the desire that had burned through every inch of me. Her eyes clung to mine and drank in every blink, every second that I closed my eyes as excitement grew within me. I stroked faster, more softly, as friction drove me higher. Just a moment, a look from her would tip me over the edge. Only a moment.

I was almost there when her tongue came out to wet her lips. I stopped all movement. I tensed my body against the urge to let go and held my breath. When her tongue went back in her mouth, when I'd found my control once more, I spoke to her.

"You're denying us both, Stephanie. Do you understand that?" She nodded her head, and I moved to her, kissed her feet then her calves, before I moved up to her knees. "I could be inside of you right now."

My lips found the inner sanctum of her thighs and brushed up the sensitive skin, until I found her center. I inhaled her scent, strong now that she was aroused, now that it dripped from her emptiness. "I could have your taste on my tongue all over again."

I pushed my nose into her silky skin there, felt how wet she was with my nose, and let my lips brush over her. I'd pulled back enough for her to watch as my tongue snaked out to gather up her taste from my lips, before I sat back again. "Instead, all I get is this. And you get nothing."

I could see that she knew by now it was pointless to speak, and I gave her a smile of approval. "That's it, pet, take your punishment. The punishment you imposed on us both."

She hadn't come at all, not yet, but I'd already spent myself earlier. Though I'd driven myself close to the edge by watching her, I could now do this for hours. Take myself to that razor sharp edge before I moved away, only to wait.

I held my hand out, grazed her knees with my fingers, but frowned. My hand shook, a slight tremor; that could be a moment of emotional upheaval or something that wasn't worth thinking about. I wasn't weak, so it must been emotion. That was not necessarily weakness, it was a sign of how strong I was. I wanted her so much my hands shook, but yet, I'd denied myself that moment.

I placed my hand against her thigh, palm down, and slid it up to her hip. My eyes followed the heated path.

I stood and took her chin between my fingers. She'd been hanging there for a while now, her arms must be tired, but she didn't complain. Even her eyes showed no signs of discomfort. There was only desire and remorse.

"Next time." I placed my cheek against hers and moved my face along hers. "Next time, you'll obey."

My lips brushed over hers, not a kiss, just a fairy-touch of a whisper. She inhaled something that sounded like a sob, but she wasn't that far gone, not yet. I placed my hands on each side of the wall beside her ribs and ran my face down her chest to graze over her nipples with my lips.

Again, not a touch, just a moment where our skin brushed together. I dropped down, my fingers a brush against her skin as they moved down beside her hips. I ran my lips over her stomach, around the intriguing indentation of her belly button, before I moved lower.

You see, I didn't touch her, not really, but she knew what those touches felt like now. She knew what it felt like to have my mouth tug at her nipples, what my tongue felt like when it dipped into her belly button, how it felt to have kisses run along her lower abdomen, until I found the spot I now faced. She knew all of these things, but yet, she'd defied me. Now, she could only whimper as I brushed my lips at the point where her lower lips met.

"You really should have obeyed me, pet," I

repeated before I ran my tongue down into her folds, and then I sat back to work at my dick as her taste spread over my tongue. She was a fire, one I couldn't control, but I would do my best. That was the fun of this, after all. It wasn't necessarily that Stephanie would give me complete control, right now; it was that fight to provoke her into giving it to me.

"I'm sorry, sir." Her head went down, and she simply stood there, her hands clamped to the wall. There was nothing else she could do.

I'd smiled, she'd broken, but only a little bit. Later, when I had that contract, I'd drive her deeper, but for now, she'd given in. That was all that mattered.

I stroked faster, just the right way, as I took in her submission, at last, and I breathed in a jagged breath of satisfaction. Pleasure was one thing, satisfaction, triumph, was another. She gave me that now, and I drank in every drop of it. "Stephanie."

I groaned her name and let her watch as I found my moment at last. This was what she'd denied herself, and I kept my eyes open as release jetted from me. Her eyes went round, and she wanted to look away, but I forced out more words. "Watch."

She pulled her head up, and more came out of me as her eyes took it all in. She'd denied herself this pleasure, not the same as mine necessarily, but she had denied herself the pleasure I could give her, that I now gave to myself. This could have all been hers, every moment of my focus could have been hers, but she'd wanted to play a game.

While I applauded her effort and knew it had to be made, she also had to be punished. I saw the way her eyes devoured the sight of me, took in the evidence of my pleasure on my chest, and how her tongue came out to lick at her lips all over again. Then she bit her lip; the pointy incisor on the left took her lip into a pinch, and I didn't know if it was to hold back another plea, or if it was just to clamp down on some swell of emotion she didn't want me to see.

Either way, it was a sign. One that she didn't even know she'd made with that sharp little tooth. Overall, it wasn't important, but right now, it was. Stephanie had given in, and she knew now what control was. She'd have to fight the urge to challenge me, to play games, and she'd have to pick and choose what was worth the denial of her own gratification, because now she knew I could deny her quite happily.

Then, she'd be the only one punished, and that wasn't worth the game, at all. I stood up, swiped myself with a towel, and slowly walked toward her. "Do you want down now?"

She looked up at me, a question in her eyes. "Yes, that's all for now. You can go home now."

"But...," she didn't finish because I shook my head negatively. "Not without a contract, Stephanie."

I could see she wanted to protest, but she didn't. Good. I led her into the kitchen, where she put on her clothes, grabbed her bag, and left. I couldn't help but smirk again. She was so mad, but I knew she'd see the error of her ways once her body had calmed down. She'd be back for more.

CHAPTER 6

Emily

My hands shook as I put the car in park once I'd pulled up to my own home. He'd sent me home, like a naughty school girl who had overstepped her boundaries. I'd misbehaved, and this was my punishment. My legs squeezed together when I moved to get out of the car, and I couldn't stop a wince.

It hurt so much. But not really. Not like a blister on my foot would hurt, not that kind of annoying pain. This was a pain that begged for more, more of the same treatment that had caused it. This pain might actually be worse, now that I come to think of it. I knew that blister would heal, that the pain would go.

I pushed in through the door, put my keys and bag down, and went to throw myself down on the bed. I needed a shower, a bath, whichever, to get the chlorine from the pool off of my skin, but the thought of being naked again only made the throb between my legs worse. I groaned in frustration, turned on the sound system, and sighed as Lord Huron began to sing about how he wanted to revisit the past.

Would I change anything about the night we met, I'd wondered? I'd thought about it, the way his eyes had met mine, and I'd known. I'd been so afraid, until he looked at me. Then I knew what I was there for. I knew I was there for him. I'd smiled, despite the way my body protested, and relived it all. From the first moment he'd smiled at me, to that final smile tonight. The one that said he owned me.

I couldn't get that out of my head at all, because I knew it was true. I was his now. That whole display, the way he'd refused to go any further, the way he'd shown me what I could've had, had blown me away. I curled up on the bed, and the smile turned into a grin. I put my head under my hand and felt a slight nag of pain on my wrist. I pulled it up to my face to look at it.

I'd left the lamp beside the bed on and could see clearly that the skin wasn't marked, not really. A faint line remained from where I'd pulled against the clamps, but that would go away within an hour or two. The pain would go too. What would remain was the memory of how he'd pinned me to that wall.

It had been a thrill, and I'd been afraid, for only a moment. The fear had changed as he'd touched me, to a fear of him to a fear of myself. I'd wanted him to do things, things a woman shouldn't want a man to do. We should've been gratified at our whim, wasn't that what we're told now? Waiting, denial of gratification, that was abuse, wasn't it?

No, my brain argued, it wasn't abuse at all because I knew that denial would totally be satisfied as soon as I brought him a contract. He'd briefly given the reason that I now thought was the reason he denied me. Consent.

I had to explicitly state my consent. Now that I'd thought about it, I remembered the way he'd completely honored the line in our other contract, despite my pleas, that he not engage in penetrative sex with me. I'd wanted to save that for … something.

It hadn't been some silly notion of the right 'one". I'd just wanted to wait until I was ready. Until I knew that it was the right moment. I'd begged him more than once now. I'd already decided he was who I'd waited on for so long, and it was just a matter of consenting, quite clearly, that he was.

I was more than sure. I knew with every part of me that he was the one I'd wanted to have sex with the first time. He was the man I wanted to be the one to take my virginity. But ... a frown form between my eyebrows, wouldn't I feel that with anyone who %had aroused me? Was it really that important to have the right first time?

What if I hated him in six months? Wanted him dead? Would I still feel right about it? I laughed at myself, not because I couldn't imagine hating Dylan James, because I could; I laughed because I knew it was thoughts like this that had kept me a virgin for so fucking long. Whether I hated Dylan in a month, a week, or not at all, I knew he was the one I wanted to have intercourse with, in the fullest sense of the term. Not because he would appreciate the gift I'd given him, but because virginity was something we were born with. We should think of our first time as a gift to ourselves, not to someone else.

I was, in effect, gifting Dylan to myself. That made me laugh all over again, it was so silly, but it was true, nonetheless. Dylan's cock inside of me would be my gift to me. I'd managed to hang onto this part of me for a long time. It hadn't been taken from me, nobody had forced me to give it to them. I'd had the most out of this whole thing, now, I'd take that to Dylan and give myself the moment so many would wish they could have.

I hummed along with the song on the radio as I closed my eyes for minute and rested. I'd been so anxious all day, ready to get to the good part, and now I was tired. I had a feeling that would be a familiar feeling with Dylan. It wasn't just the physical things we did, but the way he made me think, contemplate things, before I answered or acted. I had to be sure of what it was I was doing before I did it with him. I knew that now more than ever.

I heard my phone buzz and glanced over to see it was a message from Roxie.

<Well, are you a woman yet??>

She'd put a bunch of goofy emojis behind the question, and I laughed.

<No, I was a bad girl and left the contract at home. He sent me home to think about my ways.>

I added a few silly faces of my own and

waited. She'd called me instead of texting me this time.

"What the hell is wrong with you, woman?" she laughingly asked and groaned in dismay.

"I know, I'm stupid. It was a moment of madness, what can I say?"

"You can say sorry! Girl, I've been waiting all night to hear about it, and you pussy out on me?" Roxie could be quite blunt and plain when she spoke sometimes.

"I know, I know. It was … an experiment." I finally sighed and told her the truth.

"And what did you find out from this experiment, missy?"

"That Dylan wants a contract. He won't touch me until then." I left out the part where he'd clamped me to the wall and got himself off in front of me to prove the point, but it replayed in my mind.

"From the sound of that sigh, he did more than send you home, but I'll let you keep the details to yourself. When do you see him again?"

"Tomorrow. We're supposed to go to another club. That new one that you told him about."

"Ah, good. You're going to like it." She

sounded as if she had a secret that she'd wanted to keep, and I felt my face scrunch in question.

"What does that mean?"

"Nothing," she replied, but I heard the smirk through the phone, "just that it's going to open your … well, eyes."

"I don't think my eyes can be opened any wider, Roxie. Not really," I said doubtfully, but she just laughed.

"Oh, my little love, you just don't know." That chuckle was dirty, but sexy.

"I don't, huh? What else is there to learn? Mouth goes here, fingers go there, this goes in, that comes out. It's pretty basic." Even I knew I was oversimplifying it, but what else could I say?

"You'll just have to wait and see, dearie. For now, I have to get back to work. Freddie is here, and he has some friends with him tonight. It's going to be busy. They've all got the hots for that new girl, whatever her name is."

"Angel?" I asked, pulling the name out of my memory. Dylan had mentioned her one night as we headed to the room. Apparently, he'd given her the name.

"Yeah, that's her. I thought she wouldn't last,

but she's busy proving me wrong. She's quite the little trooper."

"Good. I hope she finds what she's looking for. She seemed sweet."

"Honestly, I'm not sure she knows." Roxie sighed, said something out of range of my hearing, and then came back. "Gotta go, call you tomorrow if I have time."

I knew she would and hung up. Time for that shower.

I came back to the bed to see my phone blinking on the nightstand. I frowned as I picked it up, but then grinned when I saw it was a message from Dylan. He'd sent me a short video clip. He'd been in the shower, steam billowed around him, but I could see him there, his head back, and I had to wonder where his hand was. I couldn't see below his chest, but that looked exactly how he looked when he'd came.

I felt some response deep inside of me and groaned. "Fucking tease."

I'd calmed my body down with time, but in an instant it was back, that urge to be with him, on him, with him inside of me. I knew I wouldn't be able to sleep and decided two could play that game.

I ran it all through my mind as my fingers explored. First, they teased over my nipples, until I couldn't fight the urge to go lower. I dragged my hand down my body until I found my center and the spot that ached with need. The need to be touched became a need for more touch as I pressed into it and thought about Dylan.

I'd set up the phone to record my voice, and I knew it caught every breath, every sound I made as I sought out what he'd denied me. When it came, when pleasure bloomed through my body, almost too quickly, I let out every moment of it with my voice. I wanted him to hear what he'd denied us both.

I'd waited until it was done, when my heart calmed, and I could breathe normally again, before I sent it. I didn't think about it, not long enough to wonder what the consequences might be. Not until he didn't respond.

Had he gone to sleep already? Was he angry and that was why he didn't answer? I combed my fingers through my hair and stared down at my phone, willing it to buzz, to light up, anything. I'd slid down into the covers and had pulled them up to hide the sting of tears when I heard a fist against my door.

My eyes went wide then, and I wondered how much trouble I was in. I didn't care, though. He was there, at the door. I swiped the stupid tears away and went to answer the door. He stood there, one arm braced on the doorframe, the other hand on his hips, in jeans and a black t-shirt, no shoes, his hair sticking up in every direction.

"Where's the contract, Stephanie?" He didn't look at me; he just looked down at his bare feet.

"On the bar in the kitchen. Come in." I pulled the door open but stood behind it. I'd lost the towel in my bed when I pulled the covers over me, and I was completely naked now.

"Have you signed it?" His voice was husky, as if he was having trouble speaking, and I looked at him. His gaze, however, was still on his feet.

"Yes," I said quietly, and waited.

"Good." He stalked into the house, walked through it until he found the kitchen, and looked on the bar. He picked up the stapled paper and flipped to the back. My signature was there, in ink so bold that I could see it, even in the minimal light cast by the lamp in the stove hood. "Right. Come with me."

I took his hand, still not sure whether he was angry or just holding onto barely controlled lust.

"Dylan..."

"No, please. Don't." He walked toward the only other light in the place, the lamp in the bedroom was still on, and he tugged me along with him.

Once he found the bedroom, he sat and pulled me between his spread legs. His face went between my breasts, and I hugged him tightly to me. Was he going to be rough or gentle? Would he continue the game, or would he finally make me his? I didn't know and decided that it might be best to just let him have his way.

He moved then, stood to take off his clothes, and I sat down on the bed to watch him. Lean muscles worked in his chest as he pulled the shirt off and then pushed his pants away. "I was going to wait, but that little tease? That ... Fuck..."

His hands swiped through his hair, which didn't help the wild look at all; it made it more pronounced if anything. "I can't be held responsible for what happens once I'm between your legs, Stephanie. You know that, right?"

I sucked in a breath of air. Somehow his words were hot, not frightening, and I felt my legs relax as images pushed into my brain. "Yes, sir."

I looked up at him and waited. "I wanted to do this right, but … dammit, why did you have to send me that, Stephanie? I could have gone to sleep, I could have left you alone, untouched, for one more night, if you hadn't sent me that."

I couldn't answer him. Had I done it to provoke him? I knew I had, but I hadn't expected him to drive over here in the middle of the night. Yet, here he was, and it made total sense that he would be.

CHAPTER 7

Emily

With a fingertip, he touched my shoulder, pushed me back, and I went down. Spread sideways over the bed, I looked at him, waited. He stood there, his breath made his chest rise and fall rapidly, and his desire was more than evident. He was as hard as a rock; I could see it from where I rested with my head on the arm I'd put behind me.

I lifted an eyebrow at the same moment I lifted my right leg. I opened myself up to him. More provocation, but he was here now, and I wanted whatever he had to give me. We were both aroused enough to take whatever came next. There was no doubt on my part, at least. If he wanted to drive into me brutally, and with a helpless drive, I'd be able to take it.

Dylan closed his eyes instead and took a deep breath to calm himself. He leaned over me and pulled my other leg up. He tested the waters, and a finger gently slid along my middle, but I could see by the way his nostrils flared that he could smell my desire. He did that just to tease me.

His hands moved up, took my breasts in his palm, and he squeezed softly. I pressed up into the tight grip, always in need of more. He let them go and climbed over me. He placed a knee on each side of my legs, until his face was level with mine.

"You broke me, Stephanie. You aren't supposed to do that." He kissed each of my eyes closed and then found the left corner of my lips. "I'm supposed to break you."

He inhaled the moan I gave him at his words and opened my mouth to him. My hands went up, clasped at him, my fingers in his skin as our tongues tangled together. "Fuck, Stephanie."

He muttered against my lips on a broken sigh, before he devoured my lips. I pressed my hips up into him and felt all of my control go away from me. "Please, Dylan. I need you to make it stop."

"Oh, I will, Stephanie, but not before I make it much worse." His hand came up to torment a nipple, his mouth over mine. I'd die if he kissed me much more. Not because I couldn't breathe, but because it was too heady. The slick feel of his tongue against mine was too much.

The hand that had been on my breast moved down to run over my pussy once more, and I dipped my hips and tried to capture his finger, but he pulled it away. That's when he rolled off of me and pulled me up to his face. I straddled his head while I grasped at the headboard.

By now I knew better than to protest, or to claim embarrassment, and I rode his tongue instead. I ground my pussy down onto his face as he sucked at me, while his fingers explored me, and I took everything he gave me. I knew this was more about what he was taking. He was tasting me, the sounds I made, as he drove his tongue through my folds before he found my clit and sucked.

"Fuck, that's it, make me come, baby," I groaned gutturally, too lost to care if I sounded slutty, or stupid, any of it. My fingers gripped tighter at the headboard, and I moved in ways I knew would make me ache tomorrow, but I didn't care. I was almost, fuck, almost there.

He sucked harder just as his hands opened the globes of my ass. "Dylan..."

But I couldn't speak, not when his finger

teased at me back there. Jesus, fuck, it was just a finger pressed against me, but it set me off. My nipples became impossibly tighter, and my thighs squeezed as bliss tore through me. This wasn't the languid quickness of my first orgasm earlier. Oh no, this was an explosion so bold, so strong, I felt as if light should be blazing from every part of me.

I cried out something, I didn't know or care what. I just made sound as my body shook from the hardest orgasm I'd ever had. My body moved of its own will, it spasmed, it shook, it writhed, as the pleasure rolled over me.

When it started to slow down, Dylan sucked even harder, with a faster pace, and that finger pressed deeper, almost inside of me. It was too much, all too much, and he could make it stop if he'd just stop touching me. But I didn't want it to end, it felt too good, and I knew his face was soaked with my juices. Even I could smell it now, the smell of my desire. It made something in me ache, that smell, made me want more. Of him, of the pleasure he gave, of the whole thing. I felt as if I was going crazy, and he still hadn't fucked me yet.

"Dylan..." Again, but nothing else came; it

was a plea this time to make it stop, to make it never end, I wasn't sure, but I rode it out. When it ebbed, I slumped against the bed, on my hands and knees, my head bowed against the luxurious duvet as I fought for air.

"You will not tempt me like that again, Stephanie. Never. Do you understand?" He was behind me, his hand on my hip as he pulled me gently against his cock, his hips. I felt the length of him press between my ass, and I knew my skin was wrapped around him. He made that more than clear when he thrust up and groaned.

He wasn't inside of me, just snuggly wrapped between my skin. "Yes, sir."

I knew that was a lie even then. If this was my reward, I'd do it all over again in an hour. A sharp smack against the skin of my ass, a sting that made me groan, and I was certain of it.

"Are you sure you understand, pet?" The skin where he'd slapped me itched, it stung, but I was lost in the sensation of it. It was a pain, it ached, but I wanted more. So I didn't answer.

The left side this time, to make an impression on the opposite side. It wasn't a violent move, it wasn't done in anger; it was a command to be certain, nothing more.

"I understand, sir." Oh, if that's what disobe-
dient temptation got me, then I would lie to him
with every breath I took.

"Good." He grasped at my hips. I tensed; was
this the moment then?

He paused, long enough for me to squirm, long
enough for him to pinch my hip in response. Then,
before I could even breathe again, he was inside of
me, and I was full. At my age, with the lifetime of
activities I'd taken part in, there was little resistance, little proof that this was the first time I'd had
a man inside of me, but a twinge, a slow tug of resistance remained, and I gasped, my eyes wide open.

Was it that sliver of pain that was gone before
I knew it, or the fact that I was filled with him? I
felt as if he'd split me open, and that my body
had been invaded. I shivered as he sank deeper
inside of me. This was what I'd wanted, though,
to know nothing but him, and I knew it now.

"Sir..." I urged him. I reassured him I was
alright; I said it all with just his name.

I heard a groan behind me, and my fingers
clenched into the duvet. I used that to push
against him, to take more of him. I couldn't
believe there was more, but there was, and he

slid into me with a surprised grunt. He was still, but I was ready for him to move, ready to find out what came next, and twisted my hips against him.

I pushed up onto my elbows and concentrated. His hands were clenched on my hips, but he didn't stop my movements. He just waited, soundless now, behind me. I moved and found a pace that felt right, that felt good, and fucked him.

I wasn't sure why he'd stopped, but I didn't let that stop me. He'd catch up eventually, or he'd pull away; either way, I wasn't waiting. Even if I should. I had him now, and it was all I'd wanted it to be. Every time I moved, his silky skin stretched me, the head touched me, stroked a nerve-ending, and I gasped so many times I lost count.

I moved on him, my back arched toward the bed, working purely on instinct. His fingers clenched tighter at my hips, and I stopped. I held my breath and waited. With a deep groan, he thrust into me, deep and hard, his hips a slap against my ass. He showed me a new pace, a new level of intensity, all the while his fingers grasped tighter, until I knew I'd be bruised, but I didn't care.

Dylan slammed into me, fast, hard, deep, but each thrust was controlled. It was measured, and I could hear how he struggled to maintain his grip on reality. He didn't want to come too quickly; he wanted to wait, to bring me with him or push me over first, I didn't know, but I knew he didn't want this to end quickly.

I rearranged myself, put my head down, and pushed my hand between my legs. I found his testicles and brushed at them with my fingertips.

"No!" He barked, and I pulled my hand away. "Touch yourself, but don't touch me. Not unless you want this over in seconds."

I didn't, so I found the slippery knot of my clit and pushed into it gently with the pad of my finger. This was too much. I'd come too fast, I thought, but then, I didn't care. His pace picked up to a point that was almost brutal, but I loved it. I wanted it. I wanted him wild and unleashed. When I felt a pulse within myself, familiar but different when he was inside of me, I heard him gasp. He felt that fluttering, did he? I had no idea it would feel like that, but the surprise didn't distract me.

In fact, it felt even more spectacular than when I came without him inside of me. "Dylan…"

"Too late, baby." And he was right.

"Fuck!" I almost said the safe word. We'd forgot a condom. But he hit something in me, and the wave that had started to subside crashed all over again.

Once wouldn't hurt. And never again, I promised, but didn't say it. I couldn't, not when my mouth was open in a silent scream.

"Fuck!" he cried out behind me, and I felt a hard pulse that rolled up into me deeper, and my eyes went wide in surprise. So that's what it felt like. No wonder women liked it so much.

But then he pulled out, and the rest of his seed jetted onto my back. He'd remembered far too late. All it took was that one drop, but I should be fine.

It wasn't time for that, anyway. I was pretty regular, and knew that I'd missed my fertile period already. "It's okay."

I assured him and handed him the towel I'd dried off with earlier. He cleaned us both up, and then, he surprised me. He got under the covers with me and pulled me close.

"I don't want to get you pregnant, Stephanie. We barely know each other." He eased the sting of that when he pulled against my shoulder and rocked me against him. "I am not ready for that, and somehow, I have to think you aren't ready to give up exploring this side of you yet."

"You're right. I don't want a child any more than you do. It's not part of my plan." I smiled and pulled away. "We can't let that happen again. Do you want some juice? I have some in the kitchen."

"Yeah, that'd be nice." He smiled and sank down into the pillows, a hand behind his head to watch me as I left.

The offer of a drink was more than hospitality; it gave me a minute to run through the house and hide anything that might have escaped my earlier assault on the house. I'd hidden anything with my name on it: bills, letters, diplomas, notes, anything before I'd even left for his place. I knew he could show up at my place, as he knew where it was now, and that could sink all of my plans. I didn't want him to know who I was. I grabbed my bag, threw it in a closet, then ran into the kitchen to get two glasses of orange juice.

I took them into the bedroom with a smile and glanced at my phone on the bedside table. There wasn't a lot he could learn from that. I didn't have any letters or anything in table either, so the room was safe; I could relax.

If I ever decided to tell Dylan who I was, it would be on my terms, and I thought he would respect that. I handed him the glass of orange juice, confident that my identity would remain concealed for now.

"Thanks." He sat up, gave me a kiss, and relaxed against my pillows. "So this is what your bedroom looks like?"

"Yeah, like you, I've only just moved in. I was living in, uh, New York, until then." I'd actually spent more time in Charlotte over my life, than anywhere, but I didn't want to give him that location. That was the headquarters for the family now, and I didn't want to give him a reason to connect the two.

"You don't sound like a northern girl," he said with a grin.

"As if you'd know with that Midwestern accent of yours." I laughed and snuggled close. "I was only there for a little while. I've lived in North Carolina most of my life."

"That explains it then. I guess I can understand. And my accent isn't Mid-western. I've just been there so long, I sound like I am. My adoptive parents took me to Kansas a long time ago, and well, I guess it wore off on me." He looked away, and I knew it wasn't the right time to probe. We had time, if we so chose. For now, I decided it was best to just snuggle down with the man who had just taken my virginity and try not to text Roxie like a teenager gone mad.

CHAPTER 8

Dylan

*I*t occurred to me a long time ago that each day is a new page, a new chance to live a different life. The point in life, when the thought first occurred to me, I was depressed, moody, and riddled with guilt. The James family came along, gave me a new name, and saved me. My life became an effort to repay that kindness, while at the same time, I became a business tycoon. It was like I became two different people, a son to the people I called Mom and Dad, and a threat to those who got in my way, or the way of my business.

As I took over more of the roles my father once filled, life became the same, every single day. Occasionally, there'd be a competitor to take out, or someone who wanted to sabotage my business, but I dealt with all those problems swiftly. I didn't brood over my past anymore, or the burden of guilt that I'd hidden deep inside of me; I just lived each day.

As I woke up to the warm, soft curves of the formerly virginal Miss Stephanie, I remembered that long ago thought. She'd changed each day for me now; she'd become a reason to be curious. Curiosity was something I'd left behind, something I'd replaced with a drive to eliminate competition and to succeed. From the moment I'd laid eyes on her, she'd changed my thoughts. It was an odd realization, but it was true; I was curious. What life would I live today?

Reality came flooding back in swiftly, though. She might make me curious, amongst other things, but she was only a fling. I eased away from her and slid from her bed. For a moment, I sat on the edge of the bed while my hands scrubbed at my face. This wasn't a good idea, I knew that, but it was too late to worry about consequences. I glanced back at her sleeping form and grimaced. Already, I wanted more time with her, and that was dangerous. I didn't need the distraction.

My brain knew it, said it was logical to walk away and forget her, but I could not make my body obey on that front. Maybe my brain was a little rebellious too, I thought with a wry grin. Stephanie was sultry and far too delicious to give up just yet. When this contract was done, I'd walk away. I'd promised myself that as I went to find a bathroom. I showered and cleaned myself up as much as I could, brushed my teeth with a toothbrush I'd found amongst several that hadn't been opened yet in a drawer, and dressed before the sun had even come up.

I didn't sleep much these days, but I'd had a restful night next to Stephanie. I squashed the thought that came after and went into her kitchen. I found a pad and pen on the fridge and wrote a note. Quietly, I took it to her bedroom and left it beneath her phone. I had work to do. I headed back to my place after a stop for some drive-thru breakfast and a cup of coffee. I opened my laptop up to check my email.

My work day didn't always start in an office, especially here in South Carolina. I didn't have an office yet, not really. My mom had sent me an email, so I opened it. She'd tried to call but hadn't been able to reach me. Dad was sick, not feeling too well, and she was going to take him to the doctor. That had been yesterday; how was he today?

A stroke earlier in the year had left Dad a little worse for wear, but better off than some. It had been caught quickly and treated, so he was luckier than most. He couldn't use his right arm, and when he was tired, he slurred his words. The stroke had impacted his overall health and mental faculties. He'd forget things sometimes, and he was prone to illnesses now.

I picked up my phone and called my mom. The woman I thought of as mom, though, I no longer reminded myself that she wasn't really my mother. She'd been a mother to me when I'd needed one, and that was what mattered.

"Hi there, Mom. How are you?" I said as soon as she picked up.

"I'm alright, honey. How are you?" Her voice, always a little thin and soft, sounded tired now.

I'd tried to get her to bring in more help around the house, but she wouldn't hear of it. She didn't want Dad to think he was a burden at all, even if there were alarms on all of the doors and windows now because he'd started to wander in his sleep after the stroke. It wasn't really that he was a burden, people weren't burdens after all, but he did require more care now. She refused to have anyone in but the maid and the man they kept to take care of the heavy labor around the house.

"I'm good, Mom, real good." I couldn't hide the smile in my voice. Memories of Stephanie flitted around in my head, her smile, the soft sounds she made when she was asleep, and I couldn't help but smile. I'd called for a reason, though. "How's Dad? What's going on?"

"Oh, just a little chest cold that won't go away, Dylan. The doctor gave him some medicine that should help." I could tell by the way she tried to brush it all off that she wasn't being totally honest.

"You know I can come back if you need me, right? I'll always be available for you and Dad." I felt guilty when I said that. I had turned my phone off last night, but not because of them. I'd just wanted to be away from the constant ping of emails from the hotels we owned for a little while.

"I know, honey, you're doing a great job taking care of everything, though. You're way out there at the beach, and you don't need to worry about us. Just enjoy your time out there, won't you please? I know you're looking to expand, but Dylan, you need to take a break, honey. You work too much."

"Well, you know better than anyone else, Mom, this business doesn't create a lot of time for peace and quiet. I've found a few moments, though, don't worry."

"Hmmm." She hummed into the phone, and I could picture her face, scrunched with doubt, but then I heard her chuckle. "You might not be our biological son, Dylan, but you sure are like your dad, you know?"

I laughed softly with her and had to agree. "He taught me well. I followed his example, and I have some big shoes to fill."

My dad was well over six feet tall, and he was a muscular guy, at least, he was before the stroke. Now, he was less of the man he had been. His muscles had shrunk as he recovered from the stroke, and his back was stooped now. Overnight, he'd gone from vital and healthy, to a shadow of who he had once been. His muscles had withered over time, and that, mixed with the paralyzed arm and the slurred speech, had turned him into an old man.

My heart ached when I thought about it all,

and I had to take a deep breath. "Is he going to be alright?"

The question came out quietly, softly, a gentle demand for the truth. I deserved honesty and asked for it now.

"It could get bad, but it's being treated. He should be alright. I'll let you know, though, Dylan; I promise. I won't keep you in the dark." Her voice, always so frail, had a strength behind it when she spoke this time, and I knew she was being honest.

I'd found Dad when the stroke had started. He'd been in his office, trying to call someone, but he couldn't remember the number. He'd tried to ask me to help him, and the words had come out completely garbled. I'd known something was wrong immediately and had phoned for an ambulance. I was glad now that I'd taken part in the first aid courses all of the staff were required to take. We'd been taught the warning signs of a stroke, and it had taken a second for the signs to coalesce in my head, and I'd acted quickly.

"Okay, I may be unavailable this evening, but I'll take my other phone with me, okay? If you need me it will work." I had an old flip phone, good only for phone calls, really, and kept it on hand when I went somewhere that I didn't want to be disturbed. The only people who had the number were Mom and Dad. It wouldn't disturb me if they needed me; it was my honor and duty to be there for them.

The rest of the world could fuck right off.

"I know, son. Listen, it's time to give him his medicine, so I need to go. Please, try to have some kind of fun, won't you, son?" I could hear the worry in her voice and wanted to make it go away.

"I have, Mom, I promise. My evenings, and sometimes even the days, have been really good. Stressful sometimes, but good. Now, go see to Dad. I'll talk to you soon. Love you."

She responded with her own declaration of love and hung up. She was right, I needed to enjoy the place a little more than I had so far. Dad had worked hard at his business, and he'd worked harder to spend time with his family, but he never took time for himself. Oh, he'd go to the gym at the office, and he'd take care of his body, but he never really took time off to enjoy life for himself.

I always suspected one of the reasons they hadn't had children of their own was the fact that Dad never really stopped working long enough to make any. Which kind of felt disloyal, but it was something I'd wondered about. Neither of them talked about why they'd been childless when I came along, and it didn't feel proper to ask.

The couple had always been loving, accepting, and encouraging to me, and Mom had always been affectionate, but some things were just personal. I'd come to them as a very young teenager, but despite that, I'd felt as if I'd been with them all my life by the end of the first year. I could barely remember my former life. It was a life not worth thinking about.

I got up from my desk and went to look out of the large window in the room. The beach was in view, some distance away, but still there. I watched it for a while, and then, I went into the bedroom and changed. I put on a pair of dark blue jeans, something I very rarely wore, and a long-sleeved gray shirt.

I had plans later. I was taking Stephanie to a new club, but I'd decided to spend a little time on the beach before that. I drove the car out to a public parking area and got out. I wasn't sure what I wanted to do; it was too cold to swim, even though the sun was out, and most of the tourist attractions held little appeal to me. I started to walk, the black leather loafers on my feet weren't exactly adequate for beach walking, but I didn't mind that there was sand in my shoes.

I headed down to the firmer, but wetter, sand near the surf, and put my hands down in my pockets to keep them warm. I had to admit, the sea air was cleansing and smelled good to a boy who had spent his youth surrounded only by freshwater lakes. That was, until my adoptive parents came along and showed me the coast of California and Washington state. I'd even seen the coast along Oregon as they took me along on their travels.

After I'd graduated high school, I'd spent a few weeks up in Vancouver, Canada and had gone back since. The coast was different in each place, but it always smelled the same. The sea, for all its roiling rage, or placid, seductive calmness, always smelled like the same. It calmed me, those few times when I'd escape to it, and the effect was no different now.

A breeze picked up, and my hair blew in the wind. Time for a cut, I thought, but Stephanie loved to run her fingers through it, and I loved how she gripped at it when she came. I closed my eyes as those thoughts filled my head and heard myself groan.

Fuck, that woman was incredible. I sat on a dry patch of sand and looked out at the ocean. I saw gray waves crash and knew a storm was likely on the way. The ocean was usually quite calm here, but today it twisted and churned wildly, stirring up the sand beneath. I thought that was how I felt at the moment, like the sand being churned up by a wave of something I couldn't control.

I had to get this woman out of my system, I decided, contradicting myself. I'd wanted to know more about her; I'd wanted to spend more time with her than we'd agreed to. But that wasn't possible; it simply wasn't. Even if she made me hard as a rock with only a brief thought, she wasn't meant for me. No woman was.

I wasn't going to risk a replay of the past, and I certainly wasn't going to start a relationship I might not be around for. I had work to do, places to go, and success to maintain. A woman would only complicate that. She'd come to resent me, she'd learn to hate the things that took me away from her, and that wasn't fair.

I thought about Mom, taking care of Dad with so much love in her heart that she wouldn't let anyone else near him, and I didn't want to do that to a woman who had come to love me. I wasn't sure I was even capable of loving a woman. I'd never been in love before.

Sure, I'd loved Mom and Dad, but that was familial love. Being in love was something I'd managed to avoid completely and with good reason. I felt my eyes narrow and refocused on the waves that crashed before me. Don't think about it, I told myself, and closed my eyes.

Just enjoy the next two weeks, and then, let her go. She was only a woman, dance with her, fuck her to incredible heights, and then, let her go. Simple, uncomplicated, just the way you liked it.

Then I remembered the way she smiled with a sweet tilt at the corners of her mouth. No matter what had made her smile, something I'd said or done to give her sexual satisfaction, that sweet tilt was there. Would I ever be able to forget that?

Some odd ache filled my chest, and that made

me nervous. Even a little angry. What was wrong with me? I'd taken the woman's virginity, and now I'd turned into some kind of sap? My fingers came out of my pants and dug into the sand beneath me. Maybe that was the problem. I'd taken her virginity and hadn't really thought about it.

A woman's sexual experiences didn't matter to me. She could be an expert or totally untouched; I didn't judge them on that. But something about the fact that it had been *me* who had her first really did it for me. I'd been the only man to know her in that way, I was the only man who had fucked her; I'd brought her into the grownup world of sex.

For that matter, I'd been the first man to ever touch her anywhere. In this day and age, it was next to impossible to find someone completely ignorant about human sexuality. Stephanie had known what she wanted and what she didn't want, so she'd researched somewhere along the line. But it was me who had given her those pleasures first. It was me who had shown her what she liked and didn't like. It would be me who took her even further.

For now, at least. Later, she'd find someone

else and maybe take a new path. Something about that pissed me off, though. I didn't want to admit it, but the thought of anyone else putting their hands on her made my fingers ache to connect to that someone's face. Fuck, I was in real trouble.

I pulled my knees up and put my arms around my legs. Instinctively, I'd moved into a position of watchfulness. I'd break anyone's hands that came near her, and that wasn't me, but I had a feeling I'd already changed. I'd have to try to pull away, to keep her at a distance, but if I was protective of her, of what was mine, for now, then I was in too deep already.

CHAPTER 9

Emily

"*I*'m keeping this one." I'd watched as Dylan took a small flip phone from the collection of objects we'd placed in a basket as we walked through the metal detector at the club. It was on the outskirts of town and looked like any other anonymous building. It was nicer than Elmo's, the club where I'd met Dylan, but it was of similar style inside.

Unobtrusive, tasteful, and done with an eye to relaxation, the place could have been a spa. If there'd been spa workers offering legitimate massages, I wouldn't have been surprised. Instead, the only workers I saw were security staff, bar staff, and someone who passed with a tray of food in one hand. We walked from the entrance and in through a narrow corridor that opened to a room that was small but got the point across. You chose your destination at the beginning of the night. A small door to the left had a bathroom sign tacked to it. The only entrance then was the door on the right.

I looked at Dylan, a smile in place. It felt a little odd not to have my bag or phone, but I knew I could live without it. Why had he kept this other phone? I had to wonder but assumed it was something to do with his father. He'd left me early this morning and had called me later to tell me about his call with his mother.

That had surprised me. Not that he'd called me, but that he'd discussed something so private with me. I'd thought he'd only said anything because he wanted to prepare me if he had to go back home. Otherwise, he probably would have kept it to himself. Dylan would let little things slip through every now and then, but not often.

We'd already booked our evening here, or I'd have told him we could have stayed at home if he was so worried. I hadn't even known the phone existed until he'd pulled it from his pocket. Maybe I should say something.

I moved up beside him and pushed my head close to his. He leaned down to listen as I spoke softly. "If you need to go home, or if you'd rather we go somewhere else tonight, we don't have to stay here. This can wait."

"No, it's fine, pet. I just want to be reachable if Mom needs me, that's all." He placed a reassuring hand against my arm, and we moved up to the table where a young woman with black hair and heavily made up eyes sat. Her eyes were an unusual shade of green, almost aqua in color, and I wondered if they were contacts.

"Hi there. Have you been to Whispers before?" She gave a smile filled with perfectly straight, white teeth and looked up at us with curiosity.

"No, we haven't," Dylan answered. I let my head fall timidly in my role as his sub now. I wanted to play it perfectly in public.

"Awesome, it's your first time." She gave Dylan a wink and then sent one in my direction. I felt my cheeks flame, and I wondered if it was obvious that I'd been a virgin until last night? I knew it wasn't, but still, the comment made me blush as my body remembered the moment Dylan thrust into me for the first time.

"What we offer here is every couple's fantasy. Whether that fantasy is the opportunity to watch others, be watched, take part in group sex, or just sit back and have a drink as they explore; we have it all here. Sometimes we have more of one thing than the other, and sometimes we'll have a special new kink come in, but we try to match up people that have similar, um, interests." She gave us a rather coquettish smile, and I felt at ease at last.

"It's about the fun here, the exploration, and the satisfaction of our patrons. We have three rules: no means no at all times, no exceptions at all, and you are to treat other patrons with respect. They are not employees and should not be treated as slaves. Which brings me to the final rule, those who are staff are off limits. No sex, at any time, of any kind. Am I clear?" A very black eyebrow came up then, and we both agreed.

I bit the inside of my lip between my front teeth to smother a giggle that wanted to escape. It was a nervous giggle; it would have been a display of my innocence, my nervousness, and I didn't want to come off as a complete novice.

"So how does this work then?" Dylan asked, and we both looked up at pictures behind the woman.

"Well, you've already signed up for your memberships, and let me see," she paused and looked down at the screen of the laptop in front of her. "Yes, you're premium members, so you can wander around until you find what you like. There's no need to order a package, unless you want something specific. Then we'll have to arrange that with another couple."

"I think we'll just have a look around for tonight," Dylan said, his husky voice even a rumble from his chest.

The woman nodded and looked at her laptop, typed a few keystrokes, and then reached into a drawer. She was efficient, professional, and set us both at ease. With a cheerful smile she placed stamps on our hands, and then pressed a button on her desk. I heard a buzzing sound over by the door, and Dylan looked at the woman.

"You can go in now. Welcome to Whispers; I hope you enjoy your time here." It was only then that I saw a nameplate was pinned onto her black top. Emma was printed on the almost invisible clear plastic. The name was printed in black and against her shirt; it barely showed up.

Dylan took my hand, opened the door with his free one, and we walked into a wall of sound. People crowded a large room, painted black, with multiple colors of lights placed in different areas. A band was on the stage toward the back, and we walked toward the bar on the right.

"Hi there, what can I get you?" a young man asked, and I felt my eyes go round. He had on makeup so expertly done I felt like an amateur. He looked magnificent, and the fedora, short, black denim jeans, multi-colored suspenders, and white shirt told me the man was a character I'd like to know more about. He was obviously a male, but his face was feminine, and I found myself intrigued. Not sexually, but just on a human level.

It was only when he'd pushed himself back and forth that I realized he was on roller skates. I smiled and looked up at Dylan. "I like him."

Dylan just smiled, shook his head ruefully, and answered the bartender. "Scotch for me, and," he paused, looked at me, and I tilted my head. What would he order for me? "A screw-driver for the lady."

"Good choice," I praised him as the bartender went off to make our drinks. At least the vodka would be slightly diluted by the orange juice. I wasn't a heavy drinker and never would be.

A little alcohol wouldn't be a bad idea in this place, I decided as I looked around. There were cubicles, some open and filled with chairs and tables that screamed of VIP area, and others that were shrouded by curtains. What was happening behind those?

"You still up for this?" Dylan asked as he came up behind me, his voice in my ear. His hands moved around to my hips, and I was glad I'd put on a long white dress with black sleeves. I'd barely feel that touch if I'd had on a skirt, a shirt, and underwear beneath it. With only the thin knit of my dress and a pair of barely-there panties underneath, I felt the touch almost as if I was naked. The dress came down to my knees, and a pair of long boots covered the rest of me.

"I'm more than certain, sir. I'm eager to explore." I didn't want the touch to end, but I wanted to face him, so I turned in his arms. "I want to know … so much more."

I dropped the words down to a seductive tone and placed my fingers on his chest. "Then that's what we'll do. We won't take part in anything, but if you want that to change, just let me know. If it's acceptable, we might. I'll decide later."

"Oh?" I asked, the brat coming to life as he

spoke. I even let my left eyebrow come up a little. "And what might you find acceptable?"

"Well," he sat on a bar stool and pulled me to him. The bartender had placed our drinks on the bar and left to attend to others now. "If you see something like a woman being flogged that you can't live without watching, then we'll stop and watch. If you see a room that has an invitation for group sex on the door, well, we can watch, but I don't think you want to take part in that. Not yet, at least." He took a sip of his drink and watched me.

"I, oh, I don't know." I blinked stupidly for a moment and looked around. There must be more rooms, rooms I couldn't see yet, because I didn't see an area where things like that might be happening. I'd never thought about sex with more than one person at a time, not really. I wasn't sure I wanted it.

I did want to explore, though. "Can we walk around?"

"Of course, pet, follow me." He took my hand, his drink in the other, and we followed green arrows I'd spotted, lit up, just at the level of the ceiling. Were they exit signs? No, those were in another area. Dylan followed them, and we walked through an open door into a whole new world. Somehow, most of the sound from the band was contained in the open room behind us; it was quieter back here. I saw row after row of rooms on each side of the corridor.

An elevator told us there were three more levels to explore, if we didn't find what we wanted down here. I looked at Dylan, uncertain of what to do, and he smiled. "Come along, pet. Let's open those innocent eyes a little bit."

The first window showed an older man. He looked much like Dylan. His haircut and the arrogant tilt of his head spoke of a successful career, but he was chained to a wall, and I stopped. "Dylan?"

"Yes, pet?" he asked softly, a reassuring wall of heat beside me.

"Men like to be tied up and dominated?" I hadn't really watched any of that. I'd assumed it was something men enjoyed with other men, but it was a woman in the room, all woman. I assumed. Lesson one, don't assume, I thought to myself.

"Many men adore being dominated by a woman. Or a man, it's not always gender specific. Sometimes it's fluid, a man one day, a

woman the next. It's the domination they crave."
He spoke softly, so we wouldn't disturb those on
the other side of the glass.

I flashed a glance down the hallway and saw
some of the windows were black while others
were dimly lit. I had to guess some were
blacked out on purpose. I took a deep breath
and put my gaze back on the man. The woman
had him in her hand now, the most sensitive
part of him, and she was placing some kind of
clamp on him.

"A chastity device. He can't touch himself
with that on. It will keep him from getting hard
too, once he calms down from his current state."

"But why?" I was confused again.

"It's something we've explored slightly.
Orgasm denial as domination. It forces the sub
to focus or fail; either way, the dom will find out
what their sub is made of." Something in his tone
told me there was more to it, but I wouldn't
ask now.

Dylan tugged on my hand, and we moved to
another room. This one had a window lit by
golden light. I soon found out it was a room
filled with candles. Candles that were currently
being used to drip wax onto a very buxom

blonde by a svelte brunette. "Fuck, wouldn't that hurt?"

"Watch her, pet. Look at how her nipples go tight every time the wax comes close to her breasts." I did as he commanded and watched. It was confusing because the brunette sat on the blonde's face, but she somehow managed to avoid woman's nipples. On purpose? Was that it? She was doing it to tease the blonde.

Was it always about domination and submission, this game of sex? Oh, there was certainly a give and take to it, but I pondered it now. Could you both give, without taking? No, I decided, and moved on. It was interesting, but I was eager to see what was next.

I found a room in darkness, but there were points of light in the middle of a black wall. Small spotlights. A woman sat on the bed, but as we came up a light came on, and I saw the tip of a penis come through a hole in the wall. Kind of gross, I thought with a shiver, but then, it was also interesting. In a perfect world, free of diseases, that might have interested me, I might have wanted to try it, but I wouldn't do such a thing. We'd had to submit health certificates to be accepted, so I knew everyone else had to, but I still wondered. Would I be able to tell from a dick in the wall if the person was healthy?

Honestly, there was no real way of knowing, but I couldn't do anything about it. This was my problem with anonymous sex, it was dangerous. At least with Dylan, I knew he'd been declared clean for certain. Roxie wouldn't have let him near me, otherwise.

Then we came to a room where a woman hung from a swing. Her hands were tethered over her head, and her feet were each clamped in a vice that kept her legs spread wide. Anybody could walk in and fuck her. Anybody could do anything to her. A gag in her mouth made sure she couldn't speak. I stopped, and my pulse raced. Fuck.

Something inside of me screamed the word want. I wanted to be her. Deep down, on a level I hadn't wanted to admit existed, this was what I'd wanted. I didn't want a choice; I'd wanted to take what she had a step further and be blindfolded too. I must have made some sound, because Dylan looked at me.

"This, pet?"

"Mmm." I couldn't say anything else. I was too caught up in the woman in the swing.

CHAPTER 10

Dylan

My little innocent former virgin had just revealed something deeply hidden, I suspected. From her still, frozen response, I knew she'd even shocked herself. This caused some deep response in her, and she couldn't look away.

A man, hidden until now, came from the shadows and touched the woman's thigh. She looked down at him, but he had on a full face mask. Only his eyes and mouth were free, and he was fully clothed. Her body was contorted in the swing, but she looked to be on the plush side. It wasn't her figure that mattered, however. It was that she'd submitted herself to this. She'd chosen this for herself.

I'd heard Stephanie breathe in deeply, a quick suck of air, and waited for a further response. She was on the verge of something here, and I wanted to watch it with her. I wanted to watch her reaction.

The man didn't speak to the woman; he just looked her over and then undid the zip on his pants. He didn't even remove his clothes. He simply moved between the woman's thighs and thrust into her, his hands on her hips to hold her in place. She couldn't even squirm away. I knew she didn't want to, though, or she wouldn't have been in the swing. From the way her legs clamped and strained against the swing's ties, I knew she'd wanted to wrap her legs around him.

I felt my heartbeat increase as I watched, but it was more Stephanie's reaction that excited me. Her nails dug into my hand, and she leaned in closer to the glass. I leaned down to whisper in her ear. "Is this what you want, pet?"

"Only with you, sir." It was an automatic response, but it was also an honest one.

"Would you want that, though, to have unknown men come to you?" I wasn't jealous, just curious.

"I don't, I think the fantasy is exciting, but watching someone else do it is arousing." Her tongue came out to wet her lips before she spoke again. "I don't think I'm that brave. Or careless. Is it careless?"

She didn't look at me, she couldn't look away from the scene in the other room, but she still wanted an answer. "I suppose it is. It depends on how you look at it. Is she degrading herself, or is she taking control of her sexuality? Is she saying sex is sex, the man doesn't matter, only his dick does? That's all she needs. An anonymous dick to fill her, before she goes back to her life."

When Stephanie breathed in this time, the breath shook, and I knew my words had registered in her brain. "I don't want to share you, but in the future, one day, you might want to explore this more."

It was a gentle reminder that this wasn't forever, and I'd waited all evening to put the suggestion into her brain, into my own. We both had to be reminded that this wasn't forever. Now was the perfect time to do that. It also brought her attention back to me. Her eyes found me, and her pupils contracted, before they went wide again. I'd upset her, but she'd hidden it. Good.

She had control of her emotions, then, if not her body. She was pressed into the glass, as if she wanted to sink into the room. "We can go in, if you like."

"No. Here is good. I'm not ready. It might be too real if I go in. I want to just watch." Her hand came up, the one not in mine, and she pressed it against the glass. Her index finger crooked, and I knew it was another sign. Her body wanted what was in that room.

The man finished, he must have, because he pulled away and went through a door I hadn't noticed before. Stephanie's breathing evened out, but she didn't move. "What's next?"

"I don't know. Maybe she'll press the button in her hand so someone will come take her down, maybe there's someone who will come after." A green light lit the room, and I looked down at Stephanie. "It seems she's getting down. We can play out this fantasy, if you like, Stephanie. I can have a room prepared for you. We can pretend you don't know me."

"But it might not be you? What if someone came in through the door and it wasn't you?" Her eyes came up to mine, and I could see it was important to her that it be me. But what if it wasn't?

I'd break their kneecaps, but she needed to

know the possibility was there. I flexed my jaw for a moment, the rage at the thought that someone else might touch what was mine too powerful to brush off, but then I did. "Maybe it's something for next time then."

"Maybe so." She looked down, and I saw uncertainty on her face. "Does that disappoint you?"

"Not at all, pet. You're new to this; you have to explore. Come on, let's find out what else there is on offer here."

A different room, a room where two men were practicing their flogging skills on a woman. She was in the center of the room, chained down to a large X made just for this purpose. I saw a window to the right of the room, and I knew the other room was for observers. It spanned the entire length of the wall, so I knew the view would be unobstructed.

"Come, follow me." I took her into the empty room, flicked the lock so the occupied sign would come on, and took her to a bed. The place was concerned with hygiene, and I could smell the scent of cleaners and disinfectants as we sat. Good, I'd rather chemical smells than the risk of disease hidden by the smell of cherry blossoms.

Stephanie slipped to the floor, her head just above my knees, and we watched the threesome together. "Do you like what you see, Stephanie?"

The two men took turns, one would get to his knees, while the other flogged her nipples with a soft leather flogger. When her expression changed, or she made a noise, they'd move, switch places, and one would suck at her nipples while the other used a soft brush against her clit. This woman was red-headed, slim, with small breasts. She was beautiful, but she didn't live up to Stephanie.

Stephanie wasn't concerned with that, though, I had to guess. She was just enjoying watching the woman and the two men. "What about this?"

"This … oh my." Stephanie's response to this wasn't as visceral, it wasn't as pronounced, but she definitely liked it. She couldn't look away. "This looks like fun."

Again, I didn't think I could let another man touch her, not while she had a contract with me, but there would come a time when she wasn't beholden to that contract. I wanted to show her all there was to offer.

"I think you'd enjoy this, most women would.

Although, perhaps not the being chained down and flogged part, necessarily." I could hear amusement in my voice and smothered it. I didn't want her to think I was laughing at her.

"Maybe not. But two men? That sounds … interesting." Did that mean she was thinking ahead too? Or did she think I'd let another man near her? Fuck that.

Another woman? Sure, any time she wanted it. But a man? Fuck that. No.

"You're mine, pet. No other man will touch you while we have a contract." Let's just nip that idea in the bud. Even if I had introduced it to her.

"Oh, aren't we possessive." I placed my hand on the back of her neck and moved her head up to look at me.

"You're mine." I looked straight into those beautiful gray eyes of her, her blonde hair in soft waves around her face, and made sure it was understood that she was mine. For now.

"Yes, sir, I am." She placed her head on my knee, submissive all over again.

"Go to the window, pet. They can't see you." I wasn't sure that was true, but assumed it was dark enough to ensure she wouldn't be seen. I waited until she'd done as I commanded and gave her a new command. "Strip."

She looked back at me for a moment, uncertain. But then she turned, her hands on the fabric of her dress. Slowly, the material came up, and she stood in nothing more than her stilettos and panties. She awaited my next orders, but I was too busy enjoying the view. The heels pushed her ass up in just the right way, and her back arched out toward me as she clasped a hand around the elbow of her other arm. "Take it all off, Stephanie."

I loved the way the pale beige thong split her ass apart, but I loved the view of her naked even more. I unzipped my pants as she pushed the panties down her hips and over her ass, before they fell in the floor. The bra went next and then she bent at the waist to undo the straps of her shoes.

"No, leave those on." I loved the shoes, a light gold color that looked perfect against her skin. "Now, you watch them. I'm going to watch you."

I slid back to the pillows on the bed. "Now, there's one rule here, Stephanie. You can watch them, you can move around, but you can't look at me, and you can't touch yourself. Understand?"

She took a deep breath as she stood, one hand against the glass, before she responded, "Yes, sir."

"Good girl." I took my dick out, but I didn't touch it once it was free. For now, I wanted to just watch her watching them.

She stood there, her hand still against the glass, as the men pulled away from the woman. They moved to a table where a few devices rested and two glasses of beer. The woman hung there, and one of them brought her a glass to sip from. She drank heavily, then they moved away. For long moments they ignored her, on purpose, I knew, but Stephanie didn't.

"Is that all? Are they finished?" she asked after another long moment.

"Just wait, pet. It's not done yet."

Not long after that, the men moved toward the woman again. One took the device that hung from a wire, and the cross began to move. The woman turned upside down, then flat on her back. Each man took a side, each took a nipple in their mouth, and each put a hand between her thighs.

"Watch, Stephanie." She'd moved, twitched

away, but I told her to observe. She obeyed and stayed in place.

She squirmed, her back arched, and her hips pressed into the glass. "Do not touch yourself."

"I'm not," she protested, petulantly.

"Pet? Is that petulance?" I waited, but she submitted.

"No, sir."

"Good girl." I began to stroke myself as we watched. After a few minutes, the woman's body moved, pulled against the restraints, and one of the men moved. I flew from the bed and dropped my pants. I pushed Stephanie into the glass then, pulled her hips back, and thrust into her, condom in place this time. I'd slipped it on while I was on the bed. I had a feeling this would happen, and I wanted to be inside of her when the men took the woman.

I fucked into Stephanie at the exact moment the man planted himself inside of the masked, unknown woman in the next room. Stephanie gasped, her hands pressed into the glass, and we moved together, as we watched.

CHAPTER 11

Emily

*D*ylan fucked me, he fucked me at the same punishing pace the man fucked the woman in the other room, but it wasn't punishment to me. It was just good, so damn good. I wanted to touch my clit, but he'd told me not to touch myself. He hadn't changed that command yet.

"I want you to come, Stephanie. Come for me now. Squeeze your tight, slick pussy all around my dick."

"Sir," I gasped, tilted my hips, and found it caused a spark in my clit. The friction made it work, and I did it again. Then his cock hit some spot inside of me, in just the right way, and I was off. "Fuck."

I groaned the word as sparks flew through me, and I found my release with him, my eyes wide open as I watched the woman fly apart next door. Dylan followed me, the moment too much for both of us to resist for too long.

It took a moment to catch our breaths, but we did, and Dylan guided us back to the bed. The trio next door wasn't finished yet, but I had enough to think about. I pulled up close to him and rested my cheek against his chest. I waited for him to speak and listened to his heart. He'd talk if he wanted to.

For now, I had a lot to think about. Things to explore and more out there, far more. At least two more floors to explore. I looked up at the ceiling and wondered what took place upstairs. Would I even want to make it to the last floor? I had a feeling our time together would be up before then, anyway. This wasn't a place you visited daily, after all. It was an every now and then kind of entertainment.

"Are you alright, Stephanie?" I heard his voice as a rumble through his chest.

"I am, sir." It wasn't a lie. I was fine, physically. Emotionally? I was shook up. Maybe. A little.

I hadn't expected the way I'd respond to the woman in the swing. So many visions had danced in my head, and I wanted it, I'd craved it. Maybe not the anonymous man part. I'd want it to be Dylan, dressed up to be anonymous, but it would have to by Dylan. Even the thought that he might trick me, or someone might take his place on purpose, had caused its own little thrill.

Even now, I found it hard to breathe when I thought about it. It was so dirty, maybe even a word I hated to think, *slutty*, but it was only a fantasy, right? As long as it remained a fantasy, it would be just fine. I knew reality wasn't always as good as fantasy, even if Dylan had proved that wrong in every way, so far. He'd shown me that sometimes, reality was better.

Maybe I'd let him try. Maybe.

"Do you want to explore more or head home? Is your head full enough yet?" I heard a chuckle and looked at him.

"Well, I could explore more, but I'm tired. Maybe going home wouldn't be so bad." I put my head down on his chest.

"Your place or mine?" he asked, and I knew he meant to stay the night.

I wasn't sure that was a good idea. He'd made it clear earlier that he had no plans of renewing the contract. Well, he'd promised there'd be a day I'd be free of the contract, and that I could explore with more men then. I'd felt this odd vibe from him, though, as he'd said it. Was he angry at the thought of another man touching me?

Whatever it had meant, I wondered if another night together might be too much. I'd started to change in my thoughts about him, especially after last night. Maybe it was a stupid mistake women made, when they'd finally been with a man properly, but I might have formed some kind of attachment to him. That bothered me.

The whole idea was no-strings attached. Sex, companionship, then it was done. And here I was, on the verge of fucking it all up. I pulled up away from him and retrieved my clothes. I had to sit on the bed to put my panties on and then my bra. Before I could put the dress over my head, Dylan came to me, his arms around my waist to pull me close to his chest. He really shouldn't do that. Not if he wanted this to end.

Tenderness was the last thing I needed. I needed brusque, efficient, wham, bam, thank you, ma'am. Not sweetness, and certainly not tenderness. I swiped at a suspicious drop of moisture on the corner of my eye and tensed up.

"What's wrong, Stephanie?" I turned to him.

"Nothing. Just a stray thought. I have some

appointments in the morning, I have to get up early. Should we go back to my place? Maybe you should go home later."

I saw the way he inspected me, his eyes narrowed, but I didn't look at him. I just put on my dress, stood up, and smoothed it over my body. "You want me to go home tonight?"

"No, I just don't want to bother you in the morning. You can stay if you want to, but, well, it's pretty early."

I was lying through my teeth, and I could see he knew it. "It's alright."

I sighed softly, relieved. I didn't want to lie to him, and this was all very confusing to someone brand new. I had a feeling Dylan James would leave a pro a little confused, though. He didn't want a relationship, he wanted a contract, insisted on it, demanded one, but then, he wanted to sleep beside me; he wanted to hold me like a precious gift he never wanted to let go of. I took another deep breath and smiled.

"You ready?" He had his clothes on, and his face was inscrutable. I'd rejected his comfort, his tenderness; he must have realized that.

"Yeah, let's head out." We were soon on the

highway, and I watched the darkness pass by in a blur.

I remembered what Trent had said, how Dylan was an asshole, how he was some kind of villain, but I couldn't reconcile it with the man I knew. Sure, most of our time was spent engaging in sex, and the man definitely had secrets, but I couldn't see him as a killer, especially someone who would kill his parents. I glanced over at his profile as he drove, and I felt a smile tug at the corner of my mouth.

He was so handsome, but then some women found even genocidal maniacs handsome. Personal appeal was not an indication of sanity. He was definitely a dominant male; I didn't doubt that a bit. But cruel? No, not on purpose anyway. I thought, maybe, I'd confused him as much as he confused me.

He was always so confident, so sure of himself, but I'd seen him watch me sometimes, seen the confusion he'd quickly hidden away. I had a feeling that second contract meant far more than he cared to admit. Dylan James had a thing for me, as much as I had for him. The problem was, that wasn't supposed to happen, for either of us. We were supposed to go our separate ways after this. We'd both wanted that. In the beginning. Now? Well, now was a different matter.

I went into the bathroom once we'd reached my place, took a shower, and slid into bed to read while he took a shower of his own. I had a lot to think about, and sex wasn't on my mind. Not until he came back in the room. He'd brought a small bag in with him when he followed me into the house, and I looked at him in the blue and black flannel pajamas he had on with hunger. The pants hung low on his hips and somehow managed to give his bare chest an even more manly look.

Defined muscles covered his shoulders and biceps, and his arms were ropes of muscle. His stomach and chest were round too, but not from soft fat. Every inch of Dylan was muscle. Even his back, ass, and legs were muscular. My fingers itched to touch him, but I told my fingers to shut the fuck up and flicked to the next page of my eBook instead.

Dylan climbed into the side I'd left empty and picked up a tablet he'd brought in with him. He opened a book of his own, and I glanced over, surprised. I adored men who read, and he'd caught my attention again. I pretended to read, but I was watching him. His skin was so soft, luscious, and silky, that I wanted to taste him. I wanted to feel the silk of him in my mouth. I might have hummed.

I wasn't sure, but Dylan moved, and his body tensed, before it relaxed again. He took a deep breath and changed the page again. I glared at my screen. Surely he knew I was watching him. Why didn't he put the tablet down? I turned my book off and put my phone on the nightstand, turned off the light and rolled away from him.

Dylan turned the light off on his side, but he didn't turn the tablet off. He kept reading. I shifted around; the urge to touch him made me restless. He'd only fucked me a short while ago, but I'd wanted him again.

Dylan moved around, slid down into the covers, and a waft of his cologne reached my nose. Fuck! He smelled so good.

I thought I made another sound, and then I moved again. That was when Dylan laughed and pulled me to him. "Restless, kitten?"

He looked down at me in the harsh light from his tablet before it blinked off. I saw smugness there and wanted to smack him. "No, just tired."

I tilted my chin in defiance and closed my eyes. "I need to get up early."

"No you don't, you just wanted to get rid of me. We'll talk about that tomorrow. For now, shut up and kiss me." His grin relaxed me, and I lifted my face up to his. I wrapped my arms around his neck and breathed a happy sigh through my nose. This was too good to turn down.

"Open for me, kitten." He meant my legs, and he moved between them once I moved them apart. With a groan he ground himself against me, and was on the point of opening the buttons of my pajama top when an odd buzz filled the room. He froze, and I looked up at him.

A glance at the alarm clock showed me it was almost midnight. Who would call him that late? His mom. He rushed off of me and grabbed at the phone he'd placed on the table. "Hello? Mom? What's wrong?"

I could hear a female voice, but not the tone or words she'd said. I only heard Dylan's side of it. "Is he in ICU? Okay. Which hospital? Yeah, I'll be back as soon as I can arrange it."

His dad then. I sighed with sadness for him, not that we had to stop, and got up. I went and poured two glasses of apple juice and got my laptop. He might need it to look for flights. I had a private, family jet I could use, if my brothers or fathers didn't have it, but that would give away who I was. I wasn't willing to give that away yet.

Dylan was still on the phone when I came back in, so I set the glass on the table and went to the kitchen. If he was going to fly back tonight, he might need to eat. I made a nice sandwich for us both and cut it into two, added some pickles, olives, and extra chunks of cheese, before I went into the bedroom. He was sitting there, stunned.

"He had pneumonia. He's in ICU, his right lung collapsed." He spoke the words automatically, and I knew he needed me.

"Good, that's where he needs to be then. Are you going in the morning or tonight?" I didn't have to elaborate.

"Tonight, if I can arrange it."

"Good. Eat this." I handed him the plate of food and called an agent I knew. There was a charter agency that would probably have a plane available. I had the flight booked and paid for by the time he finished eating. "Alright, get dressed, and wake yourself up, Dylan. Your mom needs you, and you have a long flight to get through. Come on now. Snap out of this."

He looked at me, blinked, and shook himself. "I wish it was a dream."

"He's getting good care; you just have to get there to give him some support. Come on now." I put my arm around him and hugged him tight. "You can do this, Dylan. I know you can."

For a moment, he looked like he might protest, say he couldn't, but then I saw him snap out of it. "Thank you, Stephanie. Keep your phone on, alright? I'll take my car, that way you won't be disturbed, and it will be there when I come back."

"Are you sure? I don't mind taking you?" I watched him, but he looked alert now, ready to deal with this crisis.

"I'm good. I promise. I'll call you when I get there, alright? Thank you again. I will repay you."

"Oh, you will, now go." I bounced up to kiss him and waved him off. "Now go. And call me at a decent hour, sir. I need my beauty sleep."

I gave him a wink and saw him smile. He'll be alright then. I knew that as I watched him pull out and drive away. I went back to bed, saw his tablet and picked it up. Just a few short minutes ago, he'd been in my bed, about to rock my world, and now he was flying off to Kansas. Fucking Kansas.

I wanted to cry, but at the same time, I felt relief. Maybe some time apart would do us some good. It might help me get my head on straight and back in the game. I somehow doubted it, but one could hope. I turned the lights off, tried to remember if I'd locked the door, remembered I had, and wondered why I suddenly didn't feel as safe as I had when Dylan was here.

CHAPTER 12

Dylan

Stephanie really helped me out when she chartered the plane for me. I doubted I'd have found a commercial flight, even if I could afford a few dozen tickets on my own. She knew the area better than I did, so it was a relief when she took over and fixed it all for me.

My emotions were in turmoil too, I thought as the plane landed. I didn't have clothes with me, although I did at an apartment I still kept near my parents' home. I'd go there if I needed to change or if I was here long enough to need some sleep.

"Thanks, man, I appreciate it, really." The pilot came out and shook my hand.

"Take care, and here's my card if you need a flight back." The older man, in his mid-fifties with a smile that reminded me of an old Hollywood actor, Kirk Douglas, tugged his ball cap after that and went to find somebody to help him fuel up.

I went to the taxi rank, saw it was empty, and called for a cab. When I got to the hospital, it was late, and I wasn't allowed to go in to see Dad, but Mom came out to see me. She came out to the dull waiting room and sat down to hug me to her. "Thanks for coming, son."

"As if I'd have left you to deal with this on your own. How is he?" I pulled her into my arms, and she sighed heavily.

"He's not well, Dylan, and I doubt he's ever going to be. The doctor says if he makes it through the night he'll recover, but he doesn't hold out much hope." She had her head buried in my chest, but I could hear the pain in her voice.

She and Dad had been married for more than forty years. They were more than partners, they were mates, and I couldn't imagine Mom without Dad right beside her. That thought alone nearly broke me, but I maintained composure and just held her. "He's a fighter, Mom, and he won't leave you here alone, not without wringing every ounce of life out of himself that he can. Have faith in him."

"I imagine you're right, son," she said with a

quiet chuckle. "He needs me as much as I need him. He won't let that go."

Mom pulled away and looked out at the night sky behind us. "It's gone dark already. I hadn't realized. Do you want something to eat?"

"Have you eaten?" I watched her and saw she hadn't by her expression.

"I haven't had time to, and I've been so worried. I didn't want to leave him."

"I'll go find you something somewhere. Let me have your car keys, in case everything here is closed."

It was late, even if Kansas was a couple of hours behind South Carolina. The flight was short, but still, it was late, and I knew the only thing I'd find was all-night fast food joints. She liked most things, though, so I knew I'd find her something. I'd ended up getting two meals, one for each of us, and drove back to the hospital.

Mom came out to the waiting room and looked at me. "I know you're worried about your father, but something is different about you. What's going on?"

"I'm not sure what you mean," I said, laughing as I put a waffle-cut fry in my mouth. I couldn't speak if my mouth was full, right?

"I don't know, Dylan. You seem calm, much calmer than I thought you'd be."

"Good, ahem, good food will do that to you." I held up the burger in my hand, and she gave me that mom look that all moms had. I looked back at my burger and avoided her eyes.

"Well, you don't have to tell me now, son. When and if you're ready. As long as you're happy, that's all I care about." She patted my knee and finished her burger off. "I'll go back and check on him. I spoke with the nurse while you were gone. There's one doctor left on the floor. When he goes, she says she'll let you in. You'll have to wear a face mask and a gown, to keep germs off of him, but you can see him at least."

"Thanks, Mom. That would be great." I hugged her, and she went down the hall to the pink monstrosity that was the ICU in the hospital here. I'd seen it before, when Dad had his stroke. Why they chose pink, I'd never know, but it was pink all the same.

I thought about Stephanie and sent her a text. It was even later there, so I didn't bother to call. I knew she kept her phone on at night, but she turned the volume down. One buzz wouldn't wake her, but two or three might. I sent her one long message on her messenger and left it at that. I'd call her tomorrow, to check on her.

Normally, I wouldn't bother to even text a woman, but Stephanie deserved to know what was going on. She'd booked my flight here and had taken the time to make sure I was ready before I left. I remembered now that she'd fed me a sandwich before I left the house. I'd eaten the burger because I'd forgotten all about that and thought I'd should probably eat.

I laughed at myself. She was taking care of me without even realizing it, I thought. As if that had been her role all of her life, and I wondered about her family. Was that her role with them? She took care of them all day, ushered them around, and kept them all in order, like a mother hen?

Or maybe it was a former job she'd had. Either way, I knew she was used to taking control of things quietly, in the background, without acknowledgement, and it had revealed a lot about her. She'd wanted to be submissive, and I'd found it odd until I thought about it. In her daily life, she must feel as if she's always quietly in control, while also in demand. She has to do things without making a scene, without a lot of questions. The way she'd stepped in was a sign that she had a lot more control than she thought.

By being my sub, she had mirrored that situation, though. I sat back in a chair, yelped when it tilted back, and then settled when I realized it was supposed to do that. Maybe she was taking control by giving up her control. Wasn't that the circular game that was played in these situations? It made my head spin to think about it all, but it distracted me, so I chased my tail of thought for a while.

I still hadn't worked out who was really in control by the time Mom had come to get me. I thought I was, but I knew I wasn't, which meant, in the end, Stephanie really did have it all. Quite clearly, she had it all. It was a new understanding for me.

I followed Mom down the sickly pink hall and into a small room with an open door. The nurse handed me a gown, a paper facemask, and a cover for my head. Mom put on her own set and walked into the room on the right, the room where Dad was. There were machines and tubes going every which way around him, but he seemed oblivious. "He's asleep. They've given him medicine to help him breathe and some pain medication. It's all made him sleepy, but you can come in."

I sat in the chair beside the bed and took his hand in mine. "Are you going out for a little bit?"

"I'm going down to the bathroom and then to find some coffee. You know I stopped smoking years ago, but, right now…" She looked down at her hands, and I knew how stressed she was if she'd thought about smoking again.

"You can handle it, Mom. I know you can. Stay strong."

"I'll try, Dylan." She sighed again, and then she left me alone with Dad.

His hand was frail, and something nagged at me about it. His hands were always broad, strong, but now the skin was paper thin and draped over his bones as if he had no fat on his body at all. I held his left hand, and when I thought about it, I figured out what was wrong. His wedding ring was gone.

I guessed he couldn't wear it in ICU, but it seemed odd to see him without the golden band on his hand. It had always been there, and now that it wasn't, I saw just how frail his hands were. "Come on, Dad. You've got to pull through this. Mom needs you; I need you."

I was a grown man, talking to the only man who had given a young boy hope that the future would be better. He'd given me a reason to succeed, to make him proud, and I'd tried my best to do that justice. Now, the man who had always seemed bigger than life was in a hospital bed, a mere shadow of his former self.

"I wish I could make you better, you know. I'd give you twenty years of my life, if it meant I could spend a little bit longer with you, Dad. I really would."

I could be a narcissist sometimes, and I could definitely be selfish, but over the last week or so, I'd learned a lot. Sometimes doing things for others was rewarding, and not just in the sexual arena. I'd seen how Stephanie had respected and cared for me, and it hit me right in the heart how much I'd liked that.

The parents who had chosen to raise me had taught me a lot. I had to be arrogant to maintain the success the family business had. I had made bold choices and swift decisions that had sometimes meant people lost jobs, but if it meant more success for the hotel, that was what I'd aimed for.

Now, I wondered if I should have left those

jobs open and let my bank account take a slight hit. It wasn't as if I couldn't afford it. I was really getting into the introspection when Dad's hand gripped in mine.

"Dylan?" His voice was as dry as paper, and I stood up to offer him some ice chips Mom had left.

"Hi, Dad. Yeah, it's me. How are you feeling?"

"As if I've been run over by a fucking huge Mack truck," he grumbled out and tried to sit up.

"No, stay where you are, Dad. You need to rest. Here, suck on some of these." I rattled the cup at him, and he leaned back.

"That's what I wanted anyway, boy. Why are you here? Shouldn't you be in South Carolina working?"

"Well, Dad, your lung collapsed and you're in ICU, so I thought I'd best come out here and see you. Work can wait."

"Yes, it can. You're a long damn time fucking dead, that's for sure." His words were slurred, and he kept swearing. I wanted to laugh because my father never swore, so it must be the medicine, but I choked it down and spoke soberly to him.

"Don't let Mom hear you saying those words,

Dad. I can still remember what that Ivory soap she washed my mouth out with when I was eight tastes like."

"I'm grown, I can do what I want," he grumbled, and then his head turned, and he laughed. "Isn't that what all you kids say now?"

"I'm far from a kid, but yes; I suppose it is something my generation repeats often." I knew it came from that cartoon on a cable network, I'd watched it as a teenager, but hadn't seen it for a long time. A little chubby kid had said those words, on the show, when he was pretending to be out of control, and hearing the same words from Dad nearly cracked me up.

"Fuck it, I'm going to die soon, might as well have some fun, right?" The old man looked over at me and grinned. He'd lost more weight, and his skin had a sickly color to it. I wanted to say he looked healthy, fine, but he didn't.

"You'll be fine, Dad. The docs are going to pump you full of drugs, and you'll be off like a shot before you know it."

"I sure wish they'd do something for my pecker to make it go off like a shot." This was said quietly as his head dropped off to one side, and I doubted he'd remember anything about this exchange. I laughed quietly and wiped a mirthful tear from my eye. He had to wake up, there was no way I could tell Mom that Dad's last words had been about his penis.

If he did go now, though, I'd have something to laugh about for the rest of my life. It was a moment of comic relief that I'd desperately needed, and it was a shame he probably wouldn't remember when he woke up. I wasn't sure I could remind him about it either. Poor Dad, he'd die of embarrassment if I told him.

"Is he okay? Did he wake up?" Mom came in quietly and stood beside me.

"Um, yeah, he did. I think he's groggy still. He saw me, we talked for a minute, and then he just dropped off."

"That's a good sign at least. If he's fighting the medicine to wake up and talk to you, then he's got some spirit left in him. Let me talk with the nurse, then you can head home and get some rest, honey."

"I'm fine, Mom." I turned to stop her from going, but she'd left already. The room was small, the bed he was in filled most of it, and there wasn't much room to maneuver in, so I waited on her to come back.

She returned and insisted I go get some sleep. I thought I wouldn't be able to get any, but by the time I got into my now dusty apartment, I was exhausted and fell straight into bed. I dreamed about Stephanie, about watching her at the window, and how very much I'd wanted her. Even in my dreams she was selfless and comforted me. I curled around her, beneath a large oak tree as we listened to the surf roll nearby.

In the dream, I could be soft, gentle, and held her close. I might not be able to do it in real life, but I could do anything in my dreams. That included loving pretty little Miss Stephanie.

CHAPTER 13

Dylan

*D*ad was in the hospital for a week before they released him. The good news was, he'd been released. The bad news was, it would take him some time to recover fully. This time, I insisted Mom hire a private nurse to come in and give her a hand. I'd found an agency that had highly trained staff, with very good recommendations.

I'd waited for a couple days to make sure everyone was settled in, before I decided to go back to Stephanie. To South Carolina. Mom really liked the young woman who came to help, a professional young woman whose name was Mary. Mom loved her from the first moment she'd laid eyes on her and the pair got on well, so I felt comfortable leaving them.

I didn't want to say it, but I'd missed Stephanie terribly. She'd already agreed to an extra week on the contract, since I'd spent a week out of town. We'd talked on the phone every night, sometimes during the day, and I'd really come to see her as a friend and a lover. She was always there, on the other end of the line, to support me and offer me a break from the stress. I didn't tell her about it, but I'd hated being back here.

Not because of Mom or Dad, but because of my real parents, because of the rumors that had been spread about me and them. I didn't want to think about that time in my life, but people here, big city or not, couldn't let it go. My face had been on the news, in the papers, with the most salacious and awful headlines. People couldn't forget that; they weren't supposed to. Not a single person had been able to undo the damage of those headlines, not the police, not the court system, not the juvenile system that had been put in place to protect me. Not even other parents, parents who had known me.

I'd been in four foster homes before I went to the James household. Each one had dumped me, told my caseworker outrageous lies to get rid of me, but I knew it was the stares of other parents, the way they all whispered about me, that caused the foster parents to get rid of me. They couldn't handle the association of being a killer's caretaker, even if he was a kid. And not a killer at all.

My hands had bunched up so tight I'd almost crushed my phone to death. I put it down and got up from the couch I'd been sprawled on. What was I supposed to do, scream at everyone back then? Scream until someone listened to me? Nobody had, not until I'd been placed with the James family. Then I'd finally known what a family was, what affection was, and what it meant to be comforted.

It had taken them a little while, but soon, I'd learned that I wouldn't be hit or abused, I wouldn't be cast off, as I had been with everyone else. They took me in back then, and they still hung on to me today. They'd never let me go, and that was probably what had saved me from a life that nobody should have to live. They'd sheltered me, put me in a new school, and had squashed any rumors about me with threats of removing their monetary funding from the school. They made a very hefty donation each year, and the school wanted that. Rumors did not persist about it, and at last, I'd flourished.

But now, I was back, and people had started

to notice. That was why I'd stayed away so often, for so long. To avoid those rumors, to quell the problems it would cause Mom and Dad. They didn't care, they ignored it all, rose above it, but I knew, I heard the whispers, and I still wanted to bash a head or two in because of it.

Stephanie kept me calm, even if she didn't know it. The promise of what she had to give me kept me level, kept me in check, and that was the best gift she could give me right now. It meant I could be around for Mom and Dad and help them. Not just run from the rumors, like I always did.

Even after the trial, when the truth came out, people still persisted with their whispers. Sometimes, I'd wondered if they were right. I read about false memories once, and I'd wondered if I'd done something but forgotten it. I'd read about that too, how people could bury parts of their past so deep they didn't remember it at all. There'd been a proper, legal trial, though. I'd been released, free to go. Eventually, I'd stopped wondering, but at times, I felt almost *driven* to lash out at people. The men with their glares, the women with their snickers; I just wanted to crush them all.

I finally got up, picked myself up off the couch, and went to get in the cab I'd called. A quick dash through security, a long wait where I nursed a cold beer in a VIP lounge, and then I was on the plane. Stephanie was almost within reach.

I didn't want to think about my feelings toward her too much, mainly because I didn't want to have feelings for her. That wasn't supposed to happen, and I'd seen how she'd pulled away that last night we were together. Before she could push me too far away, though, I'd had that phone call. She'd propositioned me for sex, and I knew she could handle that.

Why had she pushed, though? Weren't women supposed to be clingy, and all up in your business? Stephanie wasn't like that, and I wondered. She was kind, considerate, and had been incredibly helpful to me, and that made me wonder. Did she care?

Stephanie kept her real life as private as I did. How could you have feelings for someone that you knew so little about?

I was asleep before I could finish the thought, and the plane was about to land before I woke up again. That beer had knocked me out, but I was wide awake when I walked through the gate and out the doors to find my car. It was a bit of a walk, but I found it soon enough.

Traffic was thick, but it didn't take too long to get to Stephanie's place. I pulled up and was at the door before I knew it. I could feel my heart thudding in my chest, and I felt as if my skin had crawled up tight around my body. I was excited to see her, more than I'd admit, and I couldn't wait for that door to open. I pounded on it with a little too much force, and I laughed when she opened it a crack.

"I'm home, pet!" I didn't mean it to sound the way it did, but I let it go. This was her home, not mine, but she didn't correct me.

Instead, she threw herself into my arms and wrapped herself around me. "Make me yours, Dylan. Please, sir, I need you so much."

I had the door closed and we were locked together against the wooden barrier. Her little face, so delicate and refined, was just on level with mine, and I looked directly in her eyes. How did she know this was what I'd needed the most from her?

"While this is a pretty display, pet, shouldn't you be on your knees?" I was in dom mode instantly, and she'd dropped down to the floor, eager to please.

"Thank you, sir, for coming back to me. I know you didn't have to." She looked down at my feet, and I bent slightly to pat her on the head.

"I'm glad to be back." I didn't make the mistake of saying 'home', again. "Now, run the shower and let me clean you. I want to touch every inch of you tonight."

I wanted to tell her I'd missed her, that I'd been almost lost without her, but that wasn't an admission a dom made while in active mode.

She looked up at me then, the corner of her mouth between her teeth, a question in her eyes. "Yes, on your hands and knees. Go on now. I'm going to get a drink before I join you."

I was familiar enough with the place that I found a glass and some water to suck down before we got started. I had a feeling I'd need it later.

I heard the shower go on and the way it changed when she got in. I followed quickly, dropped the suit and shoes I wore, and stepped in with her. "Good girl, pet. You know what to do now."

She was on her hands and knees, her hair soaking wet, but she ignored the splash of water on her face to kneel up to my hard cock. She'd touched me, and I'd nearly lost myself in that moment. It had been a week, over a week, too long. I hadn't even jerked off while I'd been gone. I'd just slept, took care of Mom and Dad, and worked. Now, with her small, womanly fingers wrapped around me, I could barely contain myself.

"Go easy, pet. It's been a while." A reward, an admission that I'd wanted her and only her touch.

"Yes, sir." She stroked me softly, licked me enticingly, and made a show out of every movement she made.

"Enough, pet. Stand." I'd almost exploded all over her tongue when she stroked it up the bottom of my dick, and I'd wanted this to last. I'd wanted this pain, this desire, to last longer than five minutes.

I'd washed her hair, her body, and ducked her under the water to make sure all the soap was gone. When I'd finished, I'd used the towel to dry her off, but it wasn't done perfunctorily. From the way I'd massaged her head while I washed her hair, to the long, lazy circles I used to soap her body up, and then the caress of my fingers through the towel, softly, but with more pressure in other places, I used every moment as she had done. To entice her, to make her body quicken with desire, to make sure my fingers found a nice, slick home when I'd plunged them into her when I'd dropped the towel.

"Tell me you missed me, pet." I'd pulled her back against my body in the still steamy bathroom, and she sank into me with a moan as my fingers delved into her.

I'd made sure to press my palm into the most sensitive part of her, and she'd made the most beautiful sound, a sound I could listen to forever.

"I missed you so much, sir." Her words came out as a pant, and my dick throbbed in response.

"Tell me how much you wanted me." I stroked into her sweet walls faster, deeper, until she was lost in my touch, until her hips followed the dance I set her to follow.

"I wanted you so much I could barely stand it. I went to a sex shop. I wanted to buy a vibrator, but you didn't tell me to, so I came home empty handed." The words came out as one long steam, without pause. She was lost in her own world, and I wanted to drive her deeper into it. I pulled my hands away, just as she began to keen a new sound.

"No!" she exclaimed in protest but then dropped to her knees. "I'm sorry, sir."

"You're overexcited; it's alright, Stephanie. Follow me." We went into the bedroom, and I'd instructed her to get up on the bed. I'd brought my belt in with me, and as I stared at her lovely bottom, I had to brace myself.

"On your hands and knees." She'd obeyed and put her ass high up in the air. I could see all of her. The wet glisten of her excitement caught my attention, and I stroked my finger of the juicy slit.

"You are so wet for me, kitten. You're about to get wetter." I moved away, positioned myself, and then brought the strap of leather down over her bottom, in just the right way to catch her vulva.

"Fuck! Sir!" she cried out, but the wiggle she did with her ass was one of tormented need. "More."

"I thought so." I brought the strap down again to make an X with the red welt that was already on her ass. Only slightly raised, the welt would soon itch, sting, and she'd want to scratch it. Over the vulnerable skin of her sex, she'd begin to feel a warmth that was beyond anything she could describe. I lashed at her again, almost exactly over the first mark, but a little further down.

Her body tensed, but she didn't beg me to stop; she didn't ask for more either. Hmm.

My hand soothed over the red marks, and I moved my mouth down to blow on her wet folds. A groan and a roll of her hips told me that was a welcome maneuver. I used my hand then and was rewarded when her pink skin turned red, the shape of my palm blooming on her ass.

"Again," she'd asked, her voice almost strangled off by her need.

I slapped her bottom again, closer to the sweet pussy that peeked out from between her legs. "More?"

Her hips had jerked, but now they'd rolled again. I took that as a yes and smacked her bottom again. "Fuck."

Her cry of pleasure almost broke me. I almost slid into her then, but I didn't. Instead, I walked away. "I'll be back."

I'd brought a gift or two back with me from

Kansas. A dildo and a small, short whip. It had six leather straps, the whip, and I knew she'd love their buttery soft texture. I'd put them in a carry-on bag and brought them in with me.

"Pet?" I called out to get her attention. She was still on her hands and knees, and now she turned to me, her eyes hungrier than I'd ever seen them before. "Are you ready for more?"

CHAPTER 14

Emily

I was face down on the bed, my brain already in a place of calm arousal. When Dylan asked me if I was ready for what came next, I had to look back at him. From the way his eyes went wide for a second, I knew he was surprised at my response.

I didn't do it on purpose, there wasn't a plan of how to look feral but sexy in my repertoire, but I could feel intensity emanating from my eyes. My lips parted, ready to speak, ready to kiss, ready to suck. I felt a warmth in my cheeks, and knew my skin was flushed. I must look like I was ready for the fucking of my life or to eat him alive.

"I'm ready," I'd told him, but now the intensity came from him. There was almost a fire in his eyes, a gray fire, but still, flames. I turned my face to the headboard and waited.

His fingers on my hips, a tickle as he moved his hands up to just above my ass. His nails dug in, and I gasped. It was pain, but it felt good too. The roughness of his touch excited me. I didn't want to explore why. I just knew it did, and that was all that mattered.

"I have something for you, pet." I heard the rustle of a bag and felt something like latex against my skin. What was it?

His fingers delved deep into me, and my hips jerked up. With a sigh, I let my head fall to the bed and enjoyed his attentions. But then he pulled his fingers away and something else nudged at my opening. It wasn't his cock, this was the latex he'd laid against my knee. Was it a dildo?

When he'd pushed the instrument into me, when he'd opened me with the device, I tensed. What was it? What had he put into me? I'd wanted to ask, but the contract said I was his. So I obeyed. I'd let him invade me.

"Good girl." He's patted my bottom and then the bag rustled again. Something slid out, and I'd felt something hard but soft against my skin. When he'd pulled up and I felt long strands of buttery softness against my bottom, I knew it was a flogger of some kind.

That notion was verified when he dragged the leather strips across my back and then up to my face. It was a fawn-colored flogger made of soft suede leather; even the handle was covered in the soft material. The strips were only about six inches long, a little over a quarter-inch wide. Just right for a little introduction.

My heart beat even faster in my chest as I looked at the tool. He was going to use it on me. He was going to hit me with it. I'd felt my toes curl with anticipation, and my nipples went tight. I'd accepted the part of me that grew excited over this. I didn't question it anymore; I'd just looked up at Dylan with a very happy smile.

"For me, sir?" I'd asked, and he'd nodded.

"Only you, Stephanie. Lie down now with your arms and legs out." He'd pushed his palm flat against my back and pressed down.

I did as instructed and turned my head away from him. Not because I didn't want to watch as he used the flogger on me, but because I wanted to anticipate it. I wanted it to be a surprise. I'd heard him move around, felt it as he adjusted the latex inside of me, and then he'd moved to the side of the bed again.

His finger dragged a line down my back, and I wiggled a little, just enough to let him know I was growing impatient. "Are you going to use it on me, sir?"

"When I'm ready to. When I think you're ready, pet." A moment longer and my breathing had started to calm down. I was about to give up hope that he'd use the flogger, that he'd take me to that place so many had talked about in blogs on the subject, and was about to beg him to do it when I felt the first blow.

It was gentle, just a swish of the leather over my back. Then it'd moved down to the small of my back. The next strike came at the top of my buttocks. My hips lifted to receive the blow, to ask for more. "More, sir."

I'd wanted it harder, faster.

He'd hummed, and then the next strike came. This one had more sting to it, and he'd followed it with another right after. This one stung even more, and my fingers gripped into the duvet. "More."

"I want you to spread your legs wider." His order was perfunctory, and I did as he asked. I felt the bed dip and then he was at my feet. Close enough that he could reach me, though.

This time, the strips caught me much lower. A few caught the swollen flesh between my legs, and I gasped at last. "There. Right there."

"As madam wishes," he said with a smug hint of amusement.

He started slow, a soft strike here, a harsher blow there, a stinging slap over the spot that made me gasp, and then another. Over and over then, he rained the blows of the soft leather against my silky skin, and I started to fade from the world.

At first, it was just me concentrating, trying to focus on the sensation of the leather against my skin, and the way my skin reacted to those sensations. Some places itched to be scratched and soothed; others burned, but in a way that made my clit throb for more. I tensed around the dildo inside of me, and now I knew why he'd put it there.

I came harder when he was inside of me, when I could clamp down on his rigid erection, and he wanted to give me that benefit while he did this. He was right to do it, the sensation only heightened the pleasure of it all, and I tried to pull my legs together, to add friction. He was between my legs, however, and I couldn't close them.

"Let me ease you, pet," he said and moved closer. I felt his fingers go beneath me, until his middle finger found the sweet spot. When I groaned in praise, he brought the flogger down, over the bottom of my ass. He made a sound this time, and I knew this was making him as hot as it was me.

I'd wanted to sob when he'd pulled his hand away and moved to stand over me again. The flogger came down, and the orgasm that had been right at the tip of his fingers began to ebb away. Instead, I went back to that fuzzy world where pleasure and pain mixed, became one, and I rode it to the rhythm of the flogger.

He set a pace that was easy to follow, not too fast, not too slow. I ground my hips into the bed and felt the latex inside of me shift around. The dildo provided resistance, became a touch as my body tried to find relief in its own way.

"Do you know, pet, if you keep moving like that, you'll come without me ever touching you? With just this flogger and your body, you can orgasm harder than you've ever imagined you could." He sped up the blows, until they came more quickly, and I listened to his voice.

My body was attuned to little more than the flogger and the results of my movements; it repeated the twist of my hips that made the dildo move, I ground my front into the bed to get some friction there, and I felt the first surge of the pleasure he spoke of.

"You don't even have to touch yourself, Stephanie. All you have to do is move, give yourself up to what you feel. You don't have to do what anybody tells you right now; you don't have to be strong and capable. All you have to do is move and feel."

I'd stopped breathing as he spoke to hear the words he spoke quietly, and to listen to my body. It wanted more grinding, so I ground my hips into the bed, my elbows braced on the mattress to provide stability. It was true, and I'd moaned with relief as the surge turned into a wave. A wave that shot through my body and made me clamp around the dildo inside of me.

"I'd rather watch you come apart on my dick, Stephanie, but this is beautiful. Do you know you're the most beautiful when you're coming? I can't get the image of that out of my head when we're apart. The way you give yourself up, it is incredible."

I didn't really hear him; I was too busy riding the ecstasy he'd given me. I was lost to it, and words no longer mattered. I was somewhere that humans weren't supposed to be, some kind of nirvana that others said didn't exist. But Dylan had given it to me. I knew it wasn't fast, it hadn't been a quick ride to orgasm-land, but the building of the blows, the sensations of the stings increasing each time, the way he'd paced it all out, had made me explode.

Before my climax finished, he'd moved between my legs and pulled the dildo out of me. Something else was added to the mix, some kind of suction cup that he placed over my clit, and I knew the night wasn't over. He'd used this on me before, and I went still.

The more I moved, the more I felt sensations, and right now, it was too much. "Take it off, please."

"You know I won't and can't. Not unless you really mean it."

"But, fuck, Dylan. It's too much." My hips bucked, an involuntary attempt to get away from the pulling sensation that really was too much. If I used the safe word, this would all stop, we'd go to sleep, and that would be the end of it.

I didn't want it to end, but this was a torment, a real torment, and it was almost unbearable. Until he'd slid into me and took the place of the dildo. I'd heard him put a condom on, and I knew he meant to fuck me, but, it was a little bit of a surprise. Mainly because he felt so different. His flesh yielded, but it yielded in different ways to the latex. He felt warm, hot even, when the dildo had only felt… there.

When he began to fuck me at a pace that he knew would send me over the edge again, I held onto the mattress. Suddenly, I'd become nothing but sex. A sexual tool, to fuck and be fucked, I was sexual sensation to feel and make felt, and I was the act itself.

Dylan wanted to pleasure me; he'd wanted to *make* me come, over and over, and so … he'd set about it. His fingers dug into my hips, a punishment, a pleasure that only enhanced the new world of being driven too far. With practiced ease, Dylan fucked me, stroked inside of me, every inch of me deep inside my walls, to find just the right spot.

"Fuck!" I screamed, and then, I think my clitoris exploded in that cup. "Dylan!"

It was a warning, something powerful had started, something that was almost … uncomfortable, that was almost *frightening* started to happen. My entire body shook from head to toe, and my throat closed up on a sound that wasn't a scream, but it was far more than a moan. It was totally fucking incredible, mind and body orgasm, and I tried to scream. It was too much, we'd gone too far, but as my nipples peaked into buds and felt as if they too exploded, my skin sung and my nerves danced. I didn't want to make it stop.

"Dylan…" I sighed his name as I slipped further away, my body a clench now, my fingers tore at the cover, my toes curled up until I thought they'd break, and I had to wonder if even my heart had clenched and had stopped beating. This was way more. Fuck. It was so much more than a mindless orgasm.

I didn't even realize Dylan had found his orgasm until he blew out a surprised sound. "Steph…"

And that's when I'd started to come back to the world. When he said that name. Someone's name, but not mine. To him, I was this person, this Stephanie. But my name was Emily. Something hungry in my soul wanted him to know that, but I'd clamped down on the urge. I didn't want him to know, I didn't want him to find out who my family was. It would all be over then.

A dragging sensation between my legs, and then Dylan was beside me. He pulled me close to his chest, and I'd curled into his strong arms. I needed his comfort. Something inside me felt as if it had been released, and I didn't know what it was.

"It's okay, Stephanie. An experience like that doesn't happen very often. It might never happen again, in fact. Just ride it out. You aren't done yet. Now comes the emotional part of it."

"Ughhh…" It was a sob, a sigh, I didn't know, but it wasn't a word.

"You can talk if you want to, but you don't have to. If you want to just sit there and let it all wash away, you can. It will, eventually. You'll find yourself calm, relaxed, and it will be all done." He soothed me with his hand against my hair, and he brushed the locks from my face.

I wanted to look at him, but I couldn't open my eyes. My mind still drifted, and now and then sparks would shoot up my spine or down it. My body wasn't done, not quite yet. I'd hoped he was right, that this wouldn't happen every time because all I'd wanted to do was cry, to empty my soul to him and tell him all of the problems I'd had in my life, all of the secrets I'd kept hidden from the world. Instead, I'd curled my hand tightly around his and just hung on.

CHAPTER 15

Emily

A few days later and we were sitting on the deck of a restaurant on the beach. We'd gone to look at a property Dylan was considering. So far, he'd had no luck finding a place that he could actually buy. He'd filled me in on how it had gone so far as we waited for our lunch to arrive.

"It's this family, well, one of the brothers anyway. Trent Thompson. That bastard just took a dislike to me for some reason." Dylan swirled the ice in his glass of tea and looked out at the water in the distance. "I don't get it. Why take such an interest in me?"

"I don't know," I'd murmured as I sipped my tea through a straw. I knew part of it, Trent thought Dylan had killed his parents. He hadn't elaborated much, but I knew my brother hated him.

I felt disloyal suddenly then squashed it. Trent didn't give a fuck that I'd needed time away, he didn't care that he'd treated me like the help my entire life; why should I care now? I didn't owe him my loyalty, not just because he was my blood. That fact obviously didn't mean much to him.

Dylan sighed and sat back in his chair. "You know, Stephanie, you're the only thing that's made this whole thing worth my while? The only reason I'm still trying is because you're here."

I cut my eyes up at him, shocked. He'd never admitted anything like that to me before. What did it mean? That he'd wanted this to become something … more? I'd wanted that not long ago, but now, did I? I didn't want to be a contracted mistress, a contracted sub, for much longer. I'd only given the previous signed contract to him because he'd insisted before he'd have actual sex with me.

We'd done that now, so many times, I thought with a secret smile, and I couldn't get enough of it. The point, however, was we no longer needed a contract. I'd signed two now, how many more would he need?

My mood soured a little, but the food showed

up. We didn't talk about much while we ate, just how the food tasted, and I was glad about that. I didn't want to be crabby with him, but this whole thing was a bit fucked up. I'd wanted more, I'd wanted to try for a future with him, even if I barely knew him.

I knew the important things, like how he'd treated me, even all this time later, and that he was just what I'd wanted in a man. At times, I caught myself thinking about love, but it was too soon for that, I was certain. You couldn't love someone you barely knew, could you? No, the thought was ridiculous. But sometimes, when he'd give me a certain look or a smile, when he'd make me laugh in just the right way, I'd wanted to blurt it out to him. I love you was right there on the tip of my tongue so many times, and it was there now.

Panic had flooded out the annoyance. Our time together would be over soon, and then he'd either ask to extend it, which he'd said he never did, or he'd walk away. That made my heart ache with a dull thud of pain that grew sharper with each beat. I was about to ask him, to demand he tell me what his plans were, when I glanced up and saw Trent and his wife Jesse on the beach, hand in hand.

"Fuck," I said under my breath and turned away from them.

"What's wrong, pet?" he asked and put his hand over mine. "I'll be damned. There's the bastard now. Do you know him?"

"I, not really. Can we go? My stomach is upset. It must be the food. I'm sorry." I stood, grabbed my purse, and Dylan moved to gather up his own things.

"Of course, I'll get you home with a glass of ginger ale. That will help." He put his hand on the small of my back and kissed the top of my head. It was an intimate, loving gesture, and it spoke volumes about our relationship.

I filled with dread as I felt eyes on my back. Someone was staring at me. I'd turned my head slightly and saw Trent staring right at me. Damn it all!

Our eyes caught, and I knew he knew. His jaw went hard, and he'd started to follow, but Jesse pulled him back. I owed her one for that. From the rage I saw on his face, I knew I was his target at the moment, not Dylan. I saw it there in his eyes, accusations, anger, and even a small amount of hurt. I turned away and took Dylan's hand. "Let's get out of here. That guy looks like he's trouble."

"He's the bastard that's fucking me over so hard. Can you believe it? Strolling on the beach with his wife, as if he wasn't trying to tank me before I can even get a foothold here. Fucking asshole."

Dylan's face was as hard as Trent's had been, and I'd ushered him out of the restaurant as quickly as I could. Trent had seen me with him. What would I do now? Would he call or come to the house?

No, I thought as Dylan drove me to my place. He'd send me a summons, probably in email, to meet with him in his office. That was more Trent's style; for some reason the man thought he was in charge of all of his siblings. He'd hated us all for so long, because his father had married our mother after Trent's mother had died. There'd been no affair or even a hint that anything had taken place. Trent had just hated my mother taking his mother's place in his father's life. And then we'd come along, and somehow, we'd stolen *his* father's attention. Not our father. His. Fuck him.

Once Dylan had me home, he was attentive, but he didn't drop the whole Trent thing. He'd mentioned something about a secret property that hadn't been listed yet, and how he was working with a very good realtor to take possession of the place quietly, but he didn't tell me what property it was, and I wasn't asking. As Trent's sister, I felt it was just wrong to get any kind of information from him.

When he kept at it, his animosity growing more pronounced, and his tone even more acidic, I began to wonder if I was in trouble. He really, *really* hated Trent; that was obvious. He spoke about this new property and beating my brother as if it was some life or death battle. I remembered how Trent had spoken about him and knew the 'battle' was a mutual thing.

"I don't understand any of this," I muttered quietly. "You're two grown men; what's this feud about? Did he do something to you? Or you to him? What started it?"

Dylan glared at me for a moment, but then he relaxed into the couch with me. I was sprawled out with a blanket over me, although it wasn't really that cold. It was chilly in the house, but not so bad I'd turned the heat on. I liked covering up, sue me.

Dylan fiddled with my feet and made sure the blanket was over them before he answered. "I don't really know what crawled up his ass, but something did. I took a little while to ask around politely about properties, gave myself time to learn the lay of the land around here, and started to get information about possible resorts I could take over. Trent had heard about me, I guess, and the next thing I knew, property owners refused to speak to me, and some pulled out of deals that were almost finished."

He paused, ran his hand through his dark hair, and sighed deeply. "The next thing I knew I was getting cards from realtors, saying they couldn't help me. It was Trent's card. He'd wanted me to know he'd blocked me."

"What a dick move!" I said and sat up to rest against the arm of the couch. "I would be upset too, I guess."

"He's fucked me over several times now. I don't get it; it's not like there isn't enough trade here for us both to operate, but still. He doesn't want me here."

"That just sounds stupid. Of him, I mean." I'd

corrected when he looked up at me. I'd smiled to let him know I'd meant it. "Who acts like that?"

My brother, I'd said to myself. My phone buzzed, and I'd reached for it. I didn't have to look at the screen to know it was Trent. I could almost swear I felt rage emanating from my phone. It buzzed again, another message. Then it started to ring.

"Who's that?" Dylan asked and looked at me.

"Just a relative." I dismissed. "Nobody important."

We still didn't talk about my family. I knew he didn't have any siblings, blood or adopted, but I'd kept my family a secret. It was stressful sometimes, hiding my real name and trying not to give information away about who I was and, more importantly, who my family was. But the anger he'd shown earlier, the way he'd reacted to seeing Trent.

I had to wonder if he'd use me to get back at Trent. I thought I could trust him not to, but I wasn't positive. That anger was on the verge of irrational, even if it was justified to a degree. No, it would do no good to come clean now.

A thought from a while back came to me then. I'd glanced at him, smiled, and turned the phone off. He might think Trent was using me to get to him, if he found out who I was. He might think I'd betrayed him, used sex and our contracts to get close to him, to get dirt on him to give to Trent. It was all a fight I knew I couldn't win, unless Dylan trusted me to be an honest person.

I was related to Trent, and I knew how people were. An entire family would be painted with the same brush one member of the family had been painted with. He'd probably think I was as dishonest as Trent was.

I pushed down on the couch, my energy suddenly gone. This was exhausting, and it was starting to be a game I was too tired to play. Dylan patted my feet and broke into my thoughts.

"Do you want me to go, pet? I know you aren't feeling well?" He smiled at me, a smile of acceptance, and I knew he'd cared about me on some level.

"No, you can stay. Could you get me that ginger ale you'd promised?" I smiled and put my foot on his leg.

"Yeah, I'll run down to the gas station on the corner and get you some. I saw there wasn't any in the fridge when we got back. I'll be gone ten minutes. Do you want anything else?"

"Maybe some plain chips? Something that will be easy on my tummy?" I didn't really want them, but it would make my upset tummy excuse more believable. I hated to lie in any way to Dylan, but it was necessary to get him out of there earlier. Besides, I'd lied enough already, hadn't I?

Guilt ate at me, but he didn't notice. Instead, he pecked me on the cheek and left to go to the store. While he was gone, I turned my phone on and scrolled through the messages. Trent was just a little angry. That little angry soon escalated though as a dozen text messages made my phone almost vibrate apart.

<You fucking disgraceful, dishonest, betraying bitch! What the fuck are you doing with Dylan James? Don't you know he's fucking psycho?>

I saw that one and threw my phone at the wall. Pain tore at my heart, hurt and anger pierced it, and tears streamed from my eyes. What the hell was wrong with my brother? Didn't he have any love for me at all?

It hurt reading his words, but they were what

I'd expected from him. Jesse was the only person he'd ever loved, the only one he'd ever been gentle with. I'd witnessed it when he was with her time and again, and it was incredible how different he was with her. He'd even started to be more accepting of our brothers once he'd started a relationship with Jesse. But me? I was still the outcast. The one on the fringes, the help. No better than a maid whose loyalty he obviously expected.

Well, he could fuck right off. I went in the kitchen, took down the bottle of scotch I'd added to my pantry for Dylan, and took a slug before I went to the bathroom to brush my teeth. My eyes were red, but it would only add to the lie that I was ill. I swiped a strip of toilet paper over my nose to make sure it was dry, flushed it away, and then went to arrange myself on the couch just as Dylan came in and went to the kitchen.

"Here you go, my sweet," Dylan called out as he brought me a glass of ginger ale with ice into the living room.

"Thank you, it's so sweet of you." I thanked him and sipped at the sweet soda. It was soothing to a stomach that really was upset now.

The problem was, ginger ale wouldn't soothe

the aching knot of pain in my stomach. Trent had really hurt me with his words, with the anger he'd oozed into that message. He'd wanted to hurt me, or he'd have chosen different words. My brother and I had both been well educated, so he knew how to use his words. That message was designed to let me know exactly what he thought of me.

I saw my phone in the floor and glanced at Dylan. He didn't notice it there. I got up and went to retrieve it. I kicked it into the hallway and the carpet that ran throughout most of the house muffled the noise. Dylan looked up as I headed toward the bathroom. "Poor babe."

"I'll be back in a second." I picked the phone up and tried to turn it on. Nothing happened, and I knew I'd have to buy a new one. Again. It hadn't helped to get a new number and new phone. My family had obviously got the new number anyway, somehow, and they'd find out any new number I might get. I'd still have to get a new phone, though.

With a sigh, I went to the bathroom, flushed the toilet, then plodded to the couch. He'd think I'd actually been in the bathroom at least. He'd put one of my favorite movies on while I was gone and smiled at me when I got back on the couch.

"I hope you don't mind; I really like this movie," he said as I pulled the cover over me, and he'd arranged it on my feet.

"No, it's one of my favorites too."

"Really? I wouldn't have thought you were a fan of Mad Max movies, but you're always full of surprises, aren't you?" He patted my feet, and I smiled, but it was a distracted smile.

For a minute I'd thought about asking him to go home, and I'd call him and end it, just to end the madness, but then he'd put that movie on. And he'd put the cover on my feet, as if he'd really cared about me. I didn't want to end it, I'd decided. I was infatuated, at the very least, and I didn't want to give up the one person who had made me feel as if I'd mattered. Not yet.

CHAPTER 16

Dylan

"I'm in trouble." I said to Roxie a few days later. There were only a few days left in the contract. A few days in which I had to make a decision. I already had. The new contract in the pocket of my suit jacket told me that. It was just a matter of getting it out and asking Stephanie to sign it.

"What's up?" She turned to me, a look of concern on her face.

Stephanie was in line for the bathroom, and I knew she'd be gone for a while. I took the opportunity to talk with the only woman I knew who could understand my problem. She wouldn't bullshit me, and she was Stephanie's friend. She would tell me what was best for her friend, but she wouldn't let it blur her vision of what was right and what was wrong.

"I want to extend the contract," I blurted it

out and waited. I knew she wouldn't laugh at me, but would she give me grief over it? Another contract was something I'd never done before. I'd already broken my own rule once, though; I might as well go in for another one, right?

"How long?" she asked without inflection or even a quirk of an eyebrow. She shot a glance in the direction of the women's bathroom and then brought her eyes back to me. She got it then.

This was just between us.

"A month. I've already broken my own rules. Another month should do it, I would think."

"Do what, exactly?" Her black-rimmed eyes pierced into mine, and for a moment, I felt like a school boy, one who had something very stupid.

"To get her out of my system." It sounded stupid even to me. What must it sound like to Roxie?

"Do you think that can actually happen? She's got to you, Dylan. She's under your skin." Roxie came out with both barrels and spoke the point blank truth. "If you've broken your rules for her, then you're fucked. It's that simple."

"Surely not?" I laughed off her words, but she didn't smile or even crack a chuckle.

"You're fucked. If you want to start the

contract all over again, you're fucked. I suggest you make it longer. Or chuck it out altogether and just have, I don't know, a fucking relationship with her?" Roxie's blonde head tilted, and she glared at me. "What the fuck is wrong with you?"

"Nothing. I've just, well, I've never had a relationship before. I don't know how any of this works. The contract makes sense to me, anyway, and covers my ass. I don't want claims of abuse, or worse, to be made against me. I know the contracts aren't legal, not really, but it covers my ass if allegations are made later."

"Do you really think Eh, Stephanie is that kind?" She'd stumbled over Stephanie's name but recovered quickly. I noticed it but brushed it off.

"I don't, but you never know, do you? I'm a wealthy man, with an empire to protect." I straightened my tie and gave Roxie a pointed glare.

Roxie muttered something, made to get up, but sat back down. "Do what you want, Dylan, but I think Stephanie is it for you. You can't fight that, and nothing you do will change it. You're all wrapped up in your feelings over her, and you have to acknowledge that, or you're going to fuck up something that could be really good. For you both."

Roxie did get up then and left me alone at the table. I watched her go and wondered what had upset her. I knew she was Steph's friend, but that reaction. Then I'd seen Freddie with a girl in his lap, a girl who wasn't Roxie, and knew she was hurt. She'd opened herself up to him and had taken a chance. Obviously, he'd thrown that away, and Roxie was hurting.

Wasn't that just an example of why I should have a contract? A contract meant I could walk away whenever I'd want to. Or was Freddie the example I should avoid? Throwing away a woman who cared for one who wanted what was in my pockets, not in my pants. I frowned, then scowled, and slugged down my drink.

I'd wanted to talk to Roxie to get some reassurance that the plan was a good one. What I'd got was more confusion. I'd also upset Roxie, though now I knew I wasn't the main reason for that. I'd thought it was kind of rude of Freddie to throw it back in Roxie's face, but what could you do? It was business, and that was why I'd wanted a contract.

I'd transferred money to a bank account

number Stephanie had given me already; apparently it was something the club used for all the transactions here. She'd said the money had arrived in her account, so I knew it was going through. I'd paid her, she fucked me, we'd both had a good time and that was that.

But it wasn't, my brain screamed as I patted the spot where the contract was. It was more than just a fuck. I'd wanted to know more about Stephanie. I'd wanted to know more than the fact that brown was her favorite color. I'd wanted to know more than her favorite music or her favorite food. I'd wanted to know about her political beliefs, what she'd wanted to do with the rest of her life, if she had any family.

I'd wanted to know it all. I could learn that in a month, then my curiosity would be satisfied. But would she tell me about her family? Would she tell me her ultimate goals in life, if she knew that I wouldn't be there to see her attain them?

I sat back, got the bartender's attention, then lifted my glass. A waitress came with the drink, and I'd brushed her off with a large tip. She'd only brought me a drink, but fuck it, it was only money. How did I make this right?

For both of us, because I didn't want to upset

Stephanie. She'd barely wanted to sign the last one, and I was fairly certain she'd pretended to forget the last one. That was why I'd refused to fuck her. To punish her for the lie. I needed honesty from her, and that lie had stung. Even if she'd done it because she didn't want to sign the contract. I had to have assurances I wouldn't be fucked over, didn't I?

Stephanie came back not long after, and we'd danced for a while, and I thought, not for the first time, what a perfect woman she was. I was sure she had a fault somewhere, none of us were ever perfect, but to me, she was. She was a seductive dancer, but she was also accomplished and had taught me a step or two of the more typical dances. She loved a lot of the movies that I did, and I'd even found I'd liked her musical tastes.

She could set me at ease, or help me through tension, even without sex. And then there was the sex. She never complained, she never said no, and she was always eager to explore whatever I desired. In all, she was great, and I couldn't ask for more.

Sometimes, every now and then, she'd go quiet. As if something was wrong, as if she had some kind of troubles in her life. I'd asked her, tried to get her to explain to me, so I could help talk her through it, but she'd always just given me a bright smile and say nothing was wrong. I knew there was, but I didn't want to push her too hard. Not right now.

I had my own troubles, and really, if I was only going to be with her for another month, then knowing her problems would only cause me to want to extend it again, wouldn't it? I couldn't make the contract for longer than a month. I'd be gone soon anyway, and I knew she wouldn't want to go to Kansas, or anywhere else for that matter, so it was no use extending it.

I had obligations. Problems of my own, I thought as I'd looked down at my hand. It trembled, and I'd flattened it out on her shoulder. Way too much exercise lately, and I'd promised myself I'd cut back, but I knew I wouldn't. I had to work at being healthy, that was true for everyone, and I liked to be at the peak of physical fitness. It helped me work the amount of hours I did and kept my body from breaking down.

We danced to another song, and then I took her back to my place. She loved my pool and went straight in for a swim. I had a shower and went to bed to read for a while. I soon heard her in the bathroom, and then she was in bed with me. A sweet cloud of her perfume followed her in, and I'd hugged her close to inhale the scent. It was one of the things I'd miss once I finally ended this arrangement.

I'd kissed the length of her neck and ran my hands down the black silky nightgown she had on. It was a vintage nightgown, but I loved it on her. I wasn't sure they made nightgowns like this now. It was a stretchy kind of material and cupped at her breasts as if it was a second skin. Soft lace decorated the edges and the bottom.

The material bunched beneath her breasts and swept down to her feet in a long swirl that I found irresistible. She knew I liked the style and had found a few more to add to her collection since I'd told her how much I loved this one. I didn't know when she'd found the time to do it, but she did. I guessed when I was at work.

I stopped thinking about it so that I could explore her more fully. I touched her, and then something overwhelmed me. Some emotion I couldn't name made my chest ache and my lungs all but seize up when I looked down into her trusting eyes. I didn't want to let her go, that was plain to me now, but I would have to. I didn't do relationships. Never.

Giving myself another month with her was dangerous. That was why I hadn't mentioned it to her yet. She'd touched my face and narrowed her eyes with concern.

"What's wrong, Dylan?" she asked softly in the dimly lit quiet of my bedroom. "You've been tense all night, what's wrong?"

"Nothing, pet. Just distracted, that's all." I thought about telling her about the property, the one that was almost mine, but I didn't want to bring anything negative into our relationship. I already had by mentioning Trent Thompson to her. I'd regretted dumping that on her, so I kept quiet now.

"What's got you distracted then, Dylan?" She moved, her hips brushed against mine, and she gave me a smile that said that was a reminder of what she should be paying attention to.

"Nothing worth worrying over, Stephanie." I kissed her softly and whispered in her ear. "Nothing that can keep me from you for long, anyway. Open your legs. Let me in."

I knew she loved it when I'd ordered her to open for me, and I repeated the order now. I moved down her body and made sure she understood that she had all of my attention now. Later, once we were both satisfied, and she'd fallen asleep, I went into my office.

In the light from my desk lamp I looked over the contract. It was the same as the last one, only this one had a much later date and a larger amount of money noted. Was it enough? Would she just say no? Had she had enough of me?

I'd thought about the way her thighs had clamped around my head earlier and knew she hadn't. She'd never said no when I told her I wanted to see her, and she was never too busy. Luckily, her period only lasted a few days, but even then, she'd spent time with me, satisfied me in other ways.

I'd thought Roxie's words and sat back in my chair. Was she right? Was I throwing away something that I'd regret letting go? Would another contract be an insult to Stephanie? Surely not, she had gone into this knowing it would end sooner or later. We'd been up front about what we'd wanted. Although, now that I thought about it, she'd never said what she wanted from this arrangement anymore.

She'd stopped after the second contract was

signed. Maybe that was because I hadn't mentioned a new one. Maybe she thought I wasn't going to renew the contract and had decided to let me go. It wasn't necessarily a bad thing. If she wasn't complaining, pleading for more time, then that meant she could let me go.

I didn't like that idea any more than I liked the idea of another man touching her after me. I knew it shouldn't bother me, but it did. I just didn't have a right to feelings like that. Not a man like me. I was too much of a wanderer, too free to be tied down. Or so I'd always thought.

No, a month was long enough. After that, I'd part ways with her, and that would be that. I wasn't falling in love with the woman; that would be stupid. I'd said it over and over again, I wasn't in love. I wasn't in love. She was just a fascinating woman. She was my mistress, a lover —not a girlfriend. I wasn't in love. But in the back of my head, I could hear a denial, a voice that said, *are you sure about that, big boy?*

CHAPTER 17

Emily

*T*he next day, I felt better prepared to handle whatever Trent had to throw at me. Okay, so my way of dealing with him was to block his number from my phone, and then Jesse's when he'd started in from her number. I'd gone out earlier in the morning, when Dylan left to get some work done, and had bought a new one. One that would allow me to block numbers at my own discretion. I kind of expected he'd show up at my door any time, so I stayed away from home for the rest of the day.

Dylan called at lunchtime to ask if I'd wanted to go to his place or mine tonight. I quickly told him I'd prefer to be at his place, and we set up a time to meet there. He had some work to do for the rest of the day, so I kept myself busy at shops, getting my nails done, and then finding a few things I'd need for my overnight stay. I didn't want to go home to pick up anything because I knew who'd be there waiting for me. I didn't want to face him, so I'd bought a new toothbrush and a few other things, crawled through second-hand shops until I found a vintage nightgown, in a soft peach color that I knew he'd love, and some clothes for tomorrow from a boutique I'd found hidden away in a strip of shops.

The new phone buzzed again around three, and I saw it was Kevin. I'd always been closest to Kevin, but I didn't want to talk to him either. He might want to call me something even worse than Trent had. He might want to tell me it would be alright. I didn't know; I just knew I didn't want to face any of them right now. I couldn't.

How did I explain the fact that I was with Dylan James? I could see it now, all of them sat in a boardroom, three almost identical glares aimed at me.

I'm his sub. We have a contract. I perform as his sub, and he pays me. God, that wouldn't help. I could hear the accusations that I'd degraded myself for money, which wasn't true; I was giving all of the money to charity. I didn't need it. I also hadn't degraded myself. If anything, I'd built up enough self-confidence to take what I'd wanted and to stand up for myself. If you considered avoidance a way of standing up for yourself, that is.

Maybe not, but to me, it was, and my brothers could all take a hike. I was a grown woman. I'd needed sex, the attention of a lover; I was a normal human being. The fact that it was Dylan James who I chose to do it with might upset them, but that was my business. I knew they'd also accuse Dylan of using me to get to them. They'd always forgot I was part of the empire's structure. A small chunk of it was mine too.

They'd ignore that, and the fact that Dylan had no idea who I was when we met. He couldn't be using me, because he didn't know my identity. I was sure they'd scoff that off, which would make me feel as if they'd thought I wasn't able to catch a man's eye. But I had. I'd done all of this on my own.

Alright, I was better off than most people. I had a large sum in the bank, and I didn't need to work or worry about how to pay my bills. I'd been lucky in that department, but I was doing all of this without them. I sat in my car, staring out at nothing as the sun set over the row of shops I'd stopped at just to waste some time. They'd say I'd fucked up, ruined my life, and that I'd need them to guide me, to make decisions for me.

That I'd need to come back to the fold and be at their beck and call again. I swiped at a tear as another thought rushed through my head. The text from Jesse's phone had made my heart skip for a second. She hadn't texted me in so long, and for a moment I'd thought she wanted to reach out to me. When I'd opened the text I saw the words 'fucking whore', and deleted it before I could read the rest.

It had been from Trent.

Why did everything have to be so hard with my family? With Dylan, life was easy, uncompli-cated, well … kind of. I knew our time was almost up, but he didn't act like it was. He hadn't even mentioned it, and I took that to mean he might want to carry on. I hadn't mentioned it because I'd wanted a real relationship with him. No more contract nonsense, just us, seeing what would happen if we made a go of it.

Perhaps that was the stupidest move I'd made so far, but I didn't regret it. I didn't regret any of the things I'd done with Dylan. He gave me so much and not just pleasure. He made me feel normal, as if I had a purpose and meaning for someone. As if he needed me to make his life happy with my presence alone.

With my family, I had to give and give, my time, my patience, my knowledge; the work they considered too menial like arranging flights and surprises for their wives. The assholes couldn't remember my birthday, though. I scoffed as I thought back to what had started all of this. They'd all, my brothers and their wives, had forgot my birthday. Not a single one realized it until I pointed it out to them eventually.

No, people like that deserved no kind of loyalty from me. I checked my face in the rearview mirror, swiped a smear away, and took a deep breath. I focused on the shops in front of me. One was a jewelry store. Hmm.

I didn't remember Dylan wearing any kind of jewelry, but he did wear a watch. Maybe he'd wear a ring if I bought him one. Or a necklace. I went into the store and smiled at the eager saleswoman. Before I knew it, I'd bought an accent ring of gold chain links, a gold necklace with a crown as a pendant, and a pair of gold cuff links with tiger eyes. The ring reminded me of the chains he'd locked me in that first time, the chains that had given me my freedom. The necklace was a reminder that he was my sir, my king. And the cuff links? Well, they reminded me of the flogger. I knew he'd see the significance of each gift.

I didn't know if he'd wear them or like them, but I'd felt as if I needed to give him a solid reminder of what he was to me. To me he was all of these things and so much more. I didn't want to let him go, but if he didn't want to continue with me I'd do as he asked. It would hurt, it might rip me apart, but I'd do it.

I'd barely known the man a month, but already, he meant more to me than I'd thought possible. I'd thought I could just have sex with him, play around, have some experiences, and move on. That was how the films played at it, as if sex didn't form a bond between people. And maybe it didn't for some. If it had been someone else, besides Dylan, it might have been different. There was something about him that drew me in, and it wasn't just the sex.

We both still had secrets, depths to plumb and explore, but I felt as if I knew more about him than any other human on earth did. Perhaps his parents knew different things about him, but I knew the things about him that he wouldn't share even with them. Like how he'd liked to be the one in control, how he'd liked to whip me with just the right touch; until he'd worked me into a world I couldn't resist. I knew how he needed that, needed to watch as he gave someone else that kind of pleasure mixed with pain.

Dylan wasn't evil, even if he did like to whip women and chain them to a wall. It wasn't about force or how much he could make me scream in pain; it was about how good he made me feel. And he used pain, denial of orgasms, and pushing me over my limits to give me what I'd needed, what we'd both needed.

I drove to a Chinese restaurant, picked up some carry out food, and then drove to his place. I took the elevator up, and he was already there, in a pair of black lounge pants, a black V-neck t-shirt, with a bottle of red wine open on the table. There were even candles on the table, a deep blood red with black swirls streaked through them. I walked up to him and held my face up to him for a kiss.

"Hi there, handsome," I whispered against his lips and laughed when he bent his head to kiss me, and his arms came around me to pull me close.

"I've missed you, pet," he said out loud, and my heart skipped a beat.

"Did you?" I lifted an eyebrow and moved away to find some plates and silverware in the kitchen just behind the dining area. I came back to find him at the table, boxes open and ready to be emptied.

"Yes, I did, very much." He'd sounded a little distracted now, and I'd wanted to ask what had caused it, but I didn't. "You're here now, though."

"I am." I sat and put spoons in each box, and we'd served ourselves out of the boxes. I went quiet, my mind a whirl all over again.

He'd missed me. Did that mean he wanted to carry on? Take it a step further? Surely he wouldn't want another contract. I'd closed my eyes briefly. For some reason that caused my heart to skip a beat, but not in a good way. It was dread that made it skip, not happiness.

"What did you do today?" he asked after a bite of food. He'd looked as if he really wanted to know, and it hit me how he was the only person who'd asked me that regularly.

"Oh, I … well, I did some shopping." I went to my purse and pulled out the three fancy boxes I'd purchased at the jewelry store. "I got some things for you."

"Ah, did you now?" he asked with a gleam of happiness in his eye. I'd wondered then how often he got presents. Did he get them at all?

I slid the boxes over to him, and he looked at me quizzically. "What's this?"

"Just some things. You don't have to wear them, but … well, I wanted to get something for you. Maybe I went overboard." I'd spent a small fortune, but I wouldn't admit it. Besides, it didn't hurt my bank account at all.

I'd barely touched the money I'd received as part of my income from the hotels while I was growing up. I'd put a small dent in it lately, what with my new home, the car, and two new phones, but it was a barely noticeable dent. I'd more than make it back up by the end of the month anyway. More money would go into my account, and that would be that.

He'd looked at the boxes, looked at me with a slightly bemused frown, then opened the smallest box, the cufflinks. His eyes went wide, but then he smiled. "I love them."

"I'm glad." I had tensed up while he opened the present but relaxed now, my hands clasped together, my food forgotten.

The next box was the ring, and I saw something in his eyes and knew he was reliving the memory of that first time he'd bound me up.

"Perfect," he said and took the ring out of the box to put it on his finger. It fit his ring finger perfectly, and I'd wondered why he'd chosen to put it on that one. He'd looked down at his hand, and a flash of sadness flitted over his features before it was gone. "It's perfect. Thank you."

"You're welcome." I held my breath as he reached for the last box.

He stared at the crown for a long moment. So long that I thought maybe it had been a step too far. Did it say too much? More than I'd meant to say. I frowned and shifted around in my seat. He looked up at me, but his gaze went back to the wide box.

"This is how you see me, Stephanie?" he asked the question softly, without an accusation or hope, no emotion at all.

"Well, yes, Dylan, when we're, um, acting out

a fantasy, when you lead me into new worlds, I see you as my king, my leader, the one who commands and must be obeyed." My voice was soft, submissive, and my eyes were down on my hands. I flicked at the new gel polish on my nails, but that was one of the down sides of the sturdy polish. You couldn't fiddle with it when you were nervous.

I finally looked up and saw he'd placed the necklace around his neck, and he was watching me. "Thank you, Stephanie."

"I'm glad you like it." I could feel a blush on my cheeks. I was pleased he'd accepted the gifts and put them on.

"Nobody's ever given me jewelry before." He paused and looked at his watch. "Well, that's not true, I guess. My dad gave me this watch when I'd finished with my university degree."

"It's a nice watch." And it was, a timeless piece of art that would last generations, but it wasn't a ring or a necklace. Why didn't he have any? "Didn't you ever want to buy jewelry for yourself?"

He looked at me as if he'd felt a little bashful. "No, it never really occurred to me."

"I see." I thought it was one of the saddest

things I'd ever heard. It told me a lot about him, though. He'd focused on business, on acquiring more property, and not luxuries for himself. He had nice clothes, of course, and he was always well presented, but even that was done to maintain an image of power.

I suspected, not for the first time, that Dylan was a very lonely man who hadn't quite realized it yet. I believed he was starting to though, as he spent more time with me.

"I have something for you too, actually." He got up, went to a side table, and opened a drawer.

"You didn't have to get me anything...," I started, but my words faltered. It was an envelope, not a gift box or gift bag. An envelope.

Dread filled me, and I looked up at him. He'd just broken my heart, and he didn't even know it.

CHAPTER 18

Emily

I felt silly now, two days later, as Dylan drove us up the coast to a little place that was tucked away. An island he'd called it, but we'd been able to walk to it over a footbridge. It was a ramshackle place, apparently the place sold some kind of cake that was known around the world. I walked beside him, my heart relieved and at peace.

The envelope had not contained a contract, rather it had held information about the island. The place was so small we could walk across it in an hour. It did have a small hotel, and he'd booked us in for a night there, so close to the sea I could feel the spray from the waves that crashed against the boulders the islanders had placed around the edges as a barrier. It didn't matter if I was at the porch of the small room we'd rented, or if I was on the deck of the restaurant where the cakes were made.

"So this place was made world famous by boaters, huh?" I asked Dylan as we'd finished the pieces of multi-layered cake that deserved its reputation as a fine cake worth hunting down. It had been better than I'd expected, that was for sure.

"Yes, couples, and single-sailors, families on their way to the Bahamas in their yachts, all would come by here for this cake. It's known all over the world now." Dylan finished the last of his cake, and we sat back to watch the sun trek across the sky. The ocean was ahead of us, and the sky was clear. It was a great view.

"It must be kind of dangerous to be here when the waves are rough," I said after a while, just for something to say to end the silence.

We hadn't talked a lot, and neither of us had mentioned that the contract was up. I had noticed the sex stopped when the contract ended, but we still spent time together. I held out hope that meant something to him. I so wanted those contracts to end, and I'd learned that the night I'd given him his gifts.

He still had on the necklace and the ring. The

cuff links were for a special occasion, he'd said. I didn't know what that might be, but I'd let it go.

"It must be. The waves are rowdy right now. I'd hate to see it when they're kicking up more than this." He'd held his feet out, and I could see drops of moisture on his jeans as the waves crashed incessantly against the rocks.

I felt cold suddenly, despite the temperate. It was almost winter, but it didn't get as cold here as it did in the rest of the state, especially the mountains. I knew it wasn't the temperature or the water that had chilled me, though; it was the futility of the waves.

They'd crashed and crashed, and they'd eventually erode the coastline away, if man didn't intervene and try to preserve it. It would take a long time, unless a hurricane came through, then the island might disappear altogether. It reminded me of my relationship with Dylan far too much.

He could crush me with a single blow and walk away from me, or he could chip away, one contract at a time, until I finally gave in and let him crush me beneath his waves.

"What's wrong?" Dylan asked, and I turned to look at him.

"Nothing, just a stray thought. Shall we go to the room? I'm a little cold." I'd pulled my legs up in the lounge chair we'd moved to and wrapped my arms around them.

"Sure, if that's what you want. Or we can walk again; that might warm you up some more."

"Another walk sounds good, actually." I smiled, and we left the deck, hand in hand. After a while he pulled me closer, and I'd wrapped my arm around his waist.

"I could stay here forever," he said softly as we walked along the thin strip of beach near the end of the island. "It's just so peaceful, even with the noise from the waves."

"Maybe so, but I find it a little unsettling." He'd stopped walking, and I'd moved around to stand in front of him. I put my arms around his lean waist and put my head down on the rock wall of his chest. "Something makes it, I don't know, uncomfortable."

"Hm. Is it the isolation, do you think? I could see how it might feel like that, especially when you look toward the ocean, not back toward land." He turned me, and some of my disquiet eased.

"I think you're right. It's not so bad now.

Now, it feels more like a sanctuary from all of the hustle and bustle over there." I'd lay my head on his chest, but he pulled it up.

"To be honest, Stephanie, anywhere you are makes me feel like that." He'd looked like he'd wanted to say more, but cut it off with a sweet kiss. He'd lingered around my mouth when we'd ended the kiss, his eyes open to look into mine. "I always feel at peace with you."

"I'm glad you do." It was on the tip of my tongue to ask him, to get the dread out of the way and just ask him, but I didn't. "Do you want to go to bed?"

"No, the sun isn't down yet. We can go to the restaurant, get some drinks, and watch the sun go down if you want? I'll even get you a blanket from the room?" He still held me and that mixed with the grin on my face proved infectious and I couldn't say no.

"That sounds good. Why don't I order drinks while you get the blanket?" I let the moment go and decided to enjoy whatever this was that he was giving me.

Past experience told me there'd be no sex, not without a new contract, and I had to wonder if he was waiting on me to bring it up, or if this was a goodbye trip. Or was this a new step into a real relationship? I'd wanted it to be the last one more than I'd cared to admit, and I'd felt a little bit of relief when he'd pulled away.

I headed back to the restaurant to order a hot chocolate with mint liqueur and a scotch for him. The proprietor, an elderly man with a full head of white hair, asked where Dylan was, and I told the man he'd gone for a blanket. "Oh, we have a heater for outside, if you want me to bring it out."

"No, it's fine, really, the blanket will be enough." I smiled my thanks and walked out to the deck. I wasn't really surprised when he came out later and filled a small cast iron fire pit with wood. It wasn't close to us, but close enough that I felt the warmth from it.

"Thanks, that's great," Dylan said as the man left. We were settled in the lounge chairs again, and I had a blanket wrapped around me while we watched the sun go down.

"You're welcome," the man said, tipped his white head, and then left us in the looming darkness.

"God, it's beautiful," Dylan whispered as the

sky changed colors, and darkness slowly took over.

"It is, isn't it?" I replied and looked at him. He was looking at me.

"You meant the sunset?" he asked with a smile. "I was looking at you, cuddled up there with the fire behind you. It took my breath away."

"Oh stop it," I said and blushed. I looked back at the sky. "Watch, it's almost done, and you haven't seen it all."

"I can't look away from you, Steph." He reached out, and I gave him my hand. "You really are ... you're just, well damn ... you're just beautiful."

I looked at him, tears in my eyes, and I gave him a tight smile. "Thank you, Dylan."

"It's true, though." He took a deep sigh and finally looked at the sky to let me have time to wipe tears from my eyes. "You amaze me."

"You amaze me, sir," I said softly and felt his fingers clench around mine.

We both went quiet then and said nothing more. After our drinks were gone, we left the deck and went back to the room. Dylan held me close in the bed, and we talked about what we would do the next day. He'd wanted to stop on the drive back, show me a little shop he knew about that made furniture from driftwood. I'd drifted into sleep as he told me about the places he knew along the drive, and I dreamed about weddings and family cars.

It was a dream that disturbed me, because I knew it was impossible. Dylan had said from the start that he wasn't the marrying kind. That he wanted the contracts to keep everything businesslike. When I woke up, the memory of the way he'd looked at me nearly broke me. I went into the bathroom and turned on the faucets to hide the sob that I couldn't hold back.

With my hand over my stomach and the other over my mouth, I'd cried the pain out of my chest. It didn't help; it only gave me a headache and left me feeling drained. I got into the shower, and when I came out, wrapped in a towel, and my hair wet, I saw Dylan was awake. He'd sat up in the bed, and his eyes watched me, as if he knew I'd been crying and didn't know what to do or say to make it all better.

He'd never been in a situation like this, I knew, and he was probably trying to figure out what to do next. I looked him in the eye, mine red from tears, his filled with the pain of loss and being lost. He almost spoke, but then he didn't, for some reason. Something held him back, and I turned away to get dressed.

The moment had been there, and then it was gone. It wasn't the best way to start the day, but it was what we had. We had breakfast at the restaurant, and then we left, both of us quiet. The drive back was quiet, and dread filled me the closer we came to home. I had a feeling Trent would be there, waiting on me.

"Can I come to your place for the night?" I'd asked, and he turned with a surprised smile.

"Sure, pet. I have work to get done, but you're welcome to keep me company." He took my hand and kissed the back of it, his eyes back on the road.

"Thanks."

We got back to the apartment and took our bags up in the elevator. A short side trip to the shop he'd mentioned resulted in the purchase of a table I'd put in my hallway, which would be delivered later in the week. I felt like an intruder for some reason, as I walked around the apartment. The bare walls, still not deco-rated, reflected an emptiness, and the black colors, which had seemed modern and tasteful when I'd first come here, now seemed cold and empty.

People say a home reflects the person who lives in it. Dylan wasn't this empty, though, or cold. He could be, I knew he was ruthless in his business practices and in his dealings with others, but with me? He was as gentle as a teddy bear, unless he was being my dom. Even then, he only pushed me to the limits he knew I could handle. Only once he'd driven me past that, but it had been an incredible torment. I hadn't wanted it to end, but I'd wanted to beg him to let me go from it. I hadn't, and in the end, it was an experience I wouldn't take back.

Kind of like the whole experience I'd had with him so far. I found a blanket in a closet and wrapped it around my upper back and arms, crossed in the front to keep me warm. I walked to the windows, the huge panes of glass that gave us a view of the city. Even that spoke of distance from others, of being above it all.

Not in a snide way, but in a protective way. He could look down, see the life that was out there, but he could also keep it at bay. What had made him like that? What had drawn him into this lifestyle? Was there something broken inside of him?

I knew that the man I saw was a keeper, the kind that rarely came along. I wanted him, I wanted him sexually, emotionally, in all the ways that were possible. What I didn't want was another fucking contract.

When I'd thought he'd given me another one a few nights ago, I'd felt the world shattering around me. My hands shook when I'd opened the envelope. When I'd pulled out a brochure he'd printed for the island, I'd breathed a sigh of relief that he mistook for excitement and pleasure. I'd played along with it and tried not to shake even more as relief flooded through me.

I was still left with questions though…

"Pet? Where are you?" I heard him call from his office, and I went in to him.

"I'm here, sir. Do you need something?" I asked and went to sit on his lap.

"Just you, sweetness. Want to dance?" He smiled down at me, and I couldn't help but smile back.

"I would love to."

He picked up a remote, and a song I hadn't heard before began playing. Something by a man with a very sultry voice. He sang about how he couldn't go on without a woman who had left him, and I wondered. Why that one? He led me expertly around the empty space of his office, lit only by his desk lamp.

I watched him and quirked up when he started to sing along. His pitch was a little lower, a little sultrier than the singer's voice, and I couldn't look away. I didn't know he could sing like that.

"Wow," I said as the song ended, and he dipped me low over his arm. When I came back up, I could only stare at him. "You kept that hidden away."

"Oh, sweetheart, that's not the only secret I have." He gave me a playful wink, and I wondered what exactly he meant.

CHAPTER 19

Dylan

I'd put if off for a few days, but my self-imposed celibacy was starting to get to me. Not to mention the fear I had that she'd walk away if I didn't do something soon. I'd seen it the night she'd given me the presents. She'd been afraid of what was in that envelope, and it had put me off.

It had to be done, though. I had to offer her the contract or end this. I took a deep breath as I waited for her to come in. She'd left earlier in the day, and I'd assumed she'd gone home for a while. She had her own life, apart from me, and I didn't pry. She'd mentioned a charity of some kind, in passing, but hadn't really elaborated. Perhaps she'd done something with that.

I'd cooked dinner, steaks, baked potatoes, and a salad for us both, and it was almost done when she came in. "Hi there! Dinner's almost ready."

"It smells delicious!" I heard her say as she came into the kitchen. Dressed in a pair of tight white slacks and light blue sweater that came down to her midthigh, she'd looked soft and beautiful, as always.

She came over to kiss me and looked around. "Need help?"

"It's done. I'll bring the plates in. Do you want to bring salad dressing and silverware to the table? Oh, and open that bottle of wine?" She nodded so I went back to the steaks. I plated up the food and took it through to the dining table.

We ate happily, in silence, and shared the bottle of red wine she'd opened. By her second glass I could tell she felt a little silly and playful. I didn't want to ruin it, so I'd left the contract in the drawer. Not yet. Later. Before bed.

She was in the chair beside me to my right. I was at the end of the table and reached for her hand. She was telling me about some incident that happened at the store, something funny, but I didn't hear it. All I could see was the way her eyes lit up as she talked, and it wasn't just the flicker of flames from the candle. There was a light to her when she was happy or excited. It dimmed when she was sad, and dull when she was angry or really hurt.

How could I take that from her? I felt a tremor in the muscles of my arm, a tremor that wound its way up to my neck, and I remembered. I couldn't carry on with this. But … just a little while longer.

I'd made appropriate noises and laughed when she did, but I still didn't hear the story. My mind was still on that contract. I could have an entire month of this, if only I knew she'd sign it. From the way she'd tried to avoid the last one, and her reaction to the envelope the other day, I knew it wouldn't be easy to convince her.

She'd wanted more, and I couldn't blame her. I hadn't exactly kept it as businesslike as I'd wanted to. Normally, I'd have kept her at a distance. She'd have come over after I ate, we'd have sex, I'd use my tools on her, and we'd have more, and that would be it. My first mistake had been actually sleeping beside her.

I didn't want to admit it, but I'd loved to wake up next to her. I'd inhaled her smell and stroked her as she'd slept. I'd woken her up one morning, my dick hard and ready for her, and she'd opened her legs to me. I'd slid into her from behind and sunk into a sweet oblivion. I'd lingered inside of her, not moving at all, just enjoying the way it felt to wake up and be inside of her. She'd fallen back to sleep, I'd heard a soft snore, and that drove me to wake her up.

It had been so very sexual, the feel of her naked breast in my palm, the way her back arched into me when I fucked into her hard and swift. At the same time there'd been an air of sweet innocence to it. That had been when I knew I was in real trouble.

I had feelings for her, some anyway. I'd wanted another month to try to break that spell she had over me. It couldn't last. My parents hadn't; they'd hated each other, but they'd been unable to leave each other. Until one of them died.

I'd pushed that thought away and focused on her face. She was still talking, happy to carry on for now.

Relationships didn't last, and people only hurt you after a while. It wasn't worth it. Especially when you were, no … that wasn't worth thinking about either. Fuck, I'd looked away from her, my nerves tight as a bowstring now. I had to do it.

"Stephanie…" I began, but stopped.

"Yes, sir?" she asked, her eyes inquisitive.

"We need more wine." I got up and went for another bottle. A delay tactic, but it helped me clear my mind. "Look, we need to talk."

"Okay." Just like that the light dimmed, and she sank into herself.

I sighed deeply, but I'd started it now. I'd poured the wine and then went to the desk. I took out the folder.

It wasn't thick at all, in fact it only held two pages of paper, but I'd put it in the folder anyway. Mainly to hide it from myself.

I picked up the pen also in the drawer and took them both to her.

"I know I keep saying this is the last contract, but... Well, will you give me another month?"

It was a proposal, just not the kind she might want. It was an indecent proposal, and maybe a little cruel, but she knew that about me from the start.

"I, uh, I don't want another contract, Dylan," she finally said and looked up at me. Her eyes were full of pain and hurt, but that quickly cleared, and I saw a pair of stony gray eyes. I'd never seen them that color, and I didn't know if this was anger and rage or her pretending to be brave. "I'm done with that."

Before I could convey my thought into words, Stephanie stood up for herself, literally.

"No, I'm not. This is nonsense, Dylan!" She flicked the folder away from her side of the table, and her voice grew louder with each word. "I won't sign another one. I won't."

"Then we're done." I couldn't make it any plainer than that.

"But we don't have to be," she wailed and turned away from me to walk into the living room. I left the contract and followed her.

"Stephanie"—I went to her, took her elbow, and turned her to me—"you knew when we started this that I wasn't the kind of guy for relationships. I don't do them. Ever. I do contracts. The fact that you've lasted this long is a privilege."

Okay, that was a dick thing to say, but she had started to make me angry. The lift of her left eyebrow told me I should tread carefully, but instead, I went in like a bull in a china shop. "You've had two contract renewals. You should be on your knees sucking my dick for another offer, but instead you're arguing?"

"Excuse me?" Her head had gone back, and her eyes went round. "Shouldn't that be the other way around? You think insulting me is going to make me sign that fucking contract? Where is it?"

She left the living room and went into the dining area. She picked up the contract, looked at me, and then tore the papers in half. "This is what I think of your fucking contract, Dylan. I wanted more with you, yes. I wanted to spend time with you without a contract, this stupid weight over our heads. But you're a fucking child, aren't you? You can't fuck without words that say it's okay."

"Oh, fuck off, Stephanie," I growled the words, stung to the quick. I'd never expected her to fight back so fiercely. Tears, sure, maybe even a bout of pleading, but anger? God, she was beautiful when she was pissed off. Her cheeks were flushed, and there was a defiance in her face I'd never seen before.

This woman could have the world at her feet if she'd wanted it. How did I fix this? Wait, where was she going now?

"Stephanie?" I called out, but she didn't

answer me. She went to the hallway, toward the door. "Stephanie! Wait!"

"What? Are you going to tell me we can fix this? That you don't need your contract? Or maybe you're going to tell me to suck your dick, and you'll think about making a new one for me?" She glared daggers at me, and I dropped the hand that had reached out to grab her, to stop her from going. "Which is it, Dylan? In another month you'll want another contract, and after that, you'll ask again. Do you know what that means Mr. I Don't Do Relationships? Huh? It's a fucking relationship!"

"Stephanie...," I called, weaker this time. She was right, and I just didn't want to admit any of it. "Please. It's not childish. You know I don't do relationships."

Just tell her, my brain shouted at me, *tell her the truth. Tell her why you can't promise her more.* But I couldn't; I didn't want to. It was too shameful. Instead, I took a deep breath and looked her dead in the eye. "If you go, we're done. That's it. We're over, Stephanie."

That made her stop for a minute. She pulled her bottom lip between her teeth, and I could see her mulling something over. Whether it was a thousand ways to tell me to go fuck myself, or whether it was how to save her pride while still accepting my offer, I didn't know. I'd guessed I'd never know. She walked out of the apartment, and that was it.

Our first and only fight.

With a fit of hurt anger, I kicked the wall and knocked a hole in the drywall. Goddammit. Fuck!

I shouted the words, and then went into the dining area to fetch my glass of wine. Fine then. Fuck her. But when I sat and saw the empty plate she'd left on the table, I'd felt a sting of brand new pain. Should she drive? She'd only had two glasses of wine; I'd decided she should be fine. The refilled glass she'd left on the table mocked me. I drank the wine down and took the dishes to the kitchen.

I'd wanted to break the plates and glasses, smash everything until there was only wreckage left behind. When I was younger, before I'd learned to control my anger, I would have done just that. The entire apartment would have been destroyed. But I'd learned to swallow the anger, to control it. It was one of the reasons I didn't put pictures up on the walls; those had always been my first targets, before I'd learned to control myself. In my previous life they'd held family photos. Photos of a dysfunctional family headed for tragedy and doom, but none of us had known it when the picture was taken.

No, I couldn't submit a woman to that life, to my rage. Stephanie thought she'd seen me angry, that she'd seen my rage. She'd thought she'd seen me as dark as I could go, that she'd seen the heights of how I could control someone's pleasure and pain, how well I could dominate. I'd played with her, as soft as a kitten, even when I'd pushed her. I'd planned to keep it that way.

Now, I had visions of her on the floor, on her knees, covered in spit, tears, and my come as I fed her my cock, over and over. She'd want it, she always did, even if it was too much. It was one of the reasons I wanted her. I wanted to take her to that point, but I was afraid I'd break her totally, if I did that. She thought she wanted to go that far, but I wasn't sure she was ready for it. Not really.

And now? It didn't matter. She'd left. I picked up the bottle of wine and drank deeply. Drunk, that's what I needed. To be so drunk I'd forget her. My heart squeezed tight and I gasped, leaned over in the chair, and clutched my chest.

Was that heartbreak? Indigestion? A heart attack? It fucking hurt.

I breathed a controlled pattern, until the pain passed, and then got up to go in the living room. At least I wouldn't be near the oh so offensive contract. She'd called it childish. Maybe it was, but that didn't change the fact that I'd needed it.

Now it was all over. I should have gone after her, I thought for a moment. I should have brought her back and promised her whatever she'd wanted, everything she'd wanted. I should have promised to devote myself to her, but I hadn't. Now, I'd had too much to drink to get behind the wheel of a car. "FUCK!"

I shouted it to nobody, to an empty room, and threw the empty bottle of wine at the wall. Blearily, I saw it left a stain of wine on the wall. Fuck it. I could afford painters. I got up, went into the bedroom and slumped down into the bed. I'd reached my hands out, just a little drunk, and screamed again, only this one was just a sound of rage.

I should have been in bed with her, balls deep, making her beg for more as she screamed my name. That was what I'd had planned; I'd thought about it all damn day. But now, she was gone, probably crying in her bathtub alone. She didn't have anybody else in her life; I knew that now.

Oh, she had Roxie, but Roxie worked such odd hours; she rarely got to talk to her anymore. And since Freddie had ended his contract with Roxie, well, she'd been a bit angry too. I couldn't blame her. Life had taught us the same lessons—don't build your hopes on others. You'll lose every fucking time.

CHAPTER 20

Emily

I stared up at the ceiling in the dark. Lord Huron sang about the night he met someone he loved and lost. It burned into my brain, and I couldn't even cry. I was numb and wanted nothing more than to wallow in my pain. I'd pulled my arm up over my face to put it behind my head and felt dampness.

It was only then that I knew that I had been crying. What had I done? I'd said such cruel, hurtful things, things I didn't mean. But then, what had he done? He'd been just as hurtful, disrespectful even. Thoughts swirled, the scene played over and over again in my mind, and all I could think was had we really ended it like that? Was that the end? Was this the beginning of my painful, lonely life?

I didn't even know how I got home. One minute I was walking out angry, so fucking angry, and the next I was walking into my bedroom. Now, I was frozen, still on the bed as the song replayed. I started to think about the moments in our time together, how they related to the song.

The moment I'd seen him, when an entirely new world had opened for me in an instant. If I'd known now how it would end, would I have walked away? Would I have given up all he'd given me to miss this pain? I'd curled up into myself, a sob breaking from my throat as real tears started, the ones that were accompanied by uncontrolled sobbing.

"Fuck..." I moaned miserably. "Please. No. It can't be done."

I'd had no idea just how much a human being could hurt until now. I'd wanted to die, just to make the pain stop. But that wasn't an option; not unless a broken heart could kill you. I was too strong to do something stupid. It didn't mean I didn't long for that blackness, though. I'd tried to sleep, I'd tried to distract myself with the television later, but nothing worked. Around one am, I heard a knock on the door, and my heart skipped a beat.

It had to be, I just knew it was, and I ran to

the door. I'd kicked my shoes off at some point, but I was still in the slacks and the sweater, and my hair was a mess. I didn't care, he'd come for me. Like a white knight, my hero had come for me. He'd tell me how he'd take me in whatever capacity I'd give him, and we'd make love, make the memory of that fight disappear.

"Dylan…" I gasped, a smile on my face, but it soon melted away.

"Dylan? No, my dear sister. I'm afraid I'm not him. From the looks of your face, that's probably a good thing. Get out of the way." He pushed in the door and barged into the living room.

"What do you want, Trent?" I'd totally forgotten about him since I'd blocked his number. Then the rest of the family.

"I want you to stop seeing that smear on humanity. I want you to promise you'll end it. You are disgracing our family. How could you?"

"First of all, Trent, I'm not your employee. You don't get to barge into my house and give me orders." I stood up straight and cleared my sinuses. The tears were gone, for now, replaced with outrage. "Next, you certainly don't get to tell me who I can and can't see. I am your sister. Not your fucking maid, not your fucking wife, and certainly not your servant to order around. Got it?"

"Look, I don't care that you've decided to make a fool of yourself, but at least think about my father and your mother! How will they react knowing you're sleeping with a man who's a killer?"

I went cold all over, as if he'd doused me in ice water. I glared at him, my heart a thump in my chest. "*Your* father? **My** mother? You still aren't over that shit? He's *our* father, you prick! She's *your* stepmother. Get the fuck over it and move on!"

I was shouting by then and wondered if the neighbors could hear me. To be honest, I didn't really care. "As for those moronic rumors you persist in believing, how about you actually investigate what happened? Dylan couldn't have killed his parents; he's not capable of it!"

"For fuck's sake, Emily, are you serious? You're like some kind of Charlie Manson groupie, only it's with the parent killer instead? You'll believe anything he says, because he's nice to look at and has mesmerizing eyes? I thought you were smarter than that." Trent looked down at me, he was much taller, and sneered. His eyes, almost the same shape as mine, drilled holes into me, but I didn't buckle.

"No, Trent, I just took the time to get to know him," I said it softly, without much emotion.

"Get to know him. Fucking him isn't getting to know him, sis." He sneered that last bit, and that might be the reason I slapped him. Not the crude words, but the way he sneered sis at me, as if it was an expletive.

"I see," he said, his hand over his jaw, while I stared at him defiantly, my head up. "Fine then. It's like this—you continue with this, and you're out of the family. I'm tired of dealing with you pack of Father's brats. You're the last straw. It was tough enough dealing with Kevin and Mason, but this? This is utter betrayal, Emily. You'll regret it."

"You can't end my rights to the empire's profits. I'll be fine, Trent. I hate what you're doing to my nieces and nephews, the fact that you're taking me from them, but it can't be helped I guess." I spoke stiffly, as if it didn't hurt at all, but it did. "If you think you're man enough to over-step Dad's place and that you can ban me from the family, fine."

"Dad's already agreed to it, Emily. Stop seeing

him, or you no longer have a family." He stared at me as if he expected me to buckle and give in to the family. As I'd done a million times before. Where had it got me? Babysitting my brothers' kids, without a single happy birthday thrown my way. How many times would that happen in my life?

I could fix this all easily, tell him that it was over already, but now, it was my dignity that was at stake. My brother thought he could dictate my life. He thought that he could tell me who I could and could not spend my time. Who I could sleep with, even. No, that was done. Never again would any of them ever tell me what to do or take me for granted.

"Get out, Trent. I'll be fine without you. Just go. Fuck off and find yourself a new whipping girl. I'm done with you all." I had to bite down on my cheek to keep the tears out of my eyes, to keep the regret from making my voice shake.

"Fine. But don't come running to me if you get hurt. You've made your bed, Emily. You're going to have to lie in it now." He gave me a doubtful look, turned, and let himself out of my house.

I collapsed on the couch. I hadn't thought it

possible to feel even more pain, but I was living the reality of it. In a single night I'd lost it all. The man I was falling in love with had broken my heart, and my family had ditched me for a relationship that didn't exist anymore. If it ever really had. I'd wondered now, was it all my imagination? He'd said he wouldn't accept any other form of relationship from me, except one that involved a contract. Was that really a relationship or was it a dictatorship?

And the words he'd said. The cruel, heartless way he'd spoken to me had been shocking, to say the least. I hadn't realized he could be so hurtful. I'd never seen that side of him. Even when he had me chained to a wall, he'd been considerate, kind, but dominant. The man I'd just seen? That was petty.

I suspected Dylan had never had a relationship, not if that was his attitude through life. "I don't do relationships."

He did with his parents, but now that I thought about it, no he didn't. Sure, he knew people like Freddie and Roxie; he talked with them, and laughed, but it was an acquaintance to him, not a relationship. Did he know what a real romantic relationship was? I'd guessed I'd never find out now.

I'd picked myself up and walked to the bathroom and started to fill the bathtub. I needed to relax, to get my head straight. I'd left Dylan's in such a rush, I hadn't even thought about what it would feel like to walk into an empty house. Now, I heard every creak, every pop of the boards. When I'd walked into the kitchen, the sound of my feet slapping the floor was loud and eerie. Even the sound of the water filling the tub was too loud.

I took out a bottle of wine, poured myself a glass of Vinho Verde that Dylan had brought to me. The tub was filling, but for now, I just wanted to drink this wine and try not to cry. I knew that before long I'd be a sobbing mess again.

I did ugly cry like I'd invented it, and I was about to do some more. I could feel it coming. I'd sit there in the tub and cry stupidly, and ugly, and alone. Obviously I didn't make it to the tub.

I sobbed and turned, my head on my arms where I'd put them on the counter. My ass stuck out, but I didn't care. Nobody could see me anyway. There was no reason for shame here.

None at all, so I stood there and sobbed. After a minute, I finally noticed the same Lord Huron song was playing throughout the house and the bathtub was still running. I used a kitchen towel to wipe my face, threw it in a laundry basket when I went into the bedroom, changed the song, and went to the bathtub.

I took off the sweater I'd imagined Dylan running his hands over before he pulled it from me, and threw it at another basket. I pushed down the slacks and pushed my socks off before my panties and bra flew away somewhere. I took a deep breath and stepped into the tub.

Dylan didn't want me without a contract. I'd told him to stuff his contract. But right now? In my utter loneliness? I'd wanted nothing more than to drive over there, tape that paper back together, and sign it. I'd give him whatever he'd asked, if he'd just come back into my life. It couldn't end like this? Surely, it couldn't?

I leaned my head back against the tub and let the tears fall. How did I fix this? Could I fix it? I'd wanted to, I'd wanted to so much, but would he want to? And could I really sign that contract?

I had an opportunity here. I could totally rebuild my life, start off new, with a clearer idea of what sex was. I could have a relationship, now that I knew what that meant. I could love someone, who loved me back, and every now and then he'd tie me to a wall or to his bed and fuck me to insanity. That could happen, I thought as I put a damp washcloth over my face to hide away.

Yeah right, my brain said, *here's a picture of Dylan's face when he's between your thighs, sucking you off.* Breath shivered from my chest and desire flared to life in my groin. My body wanted Dylan still. My brain did too. Even this little part of me that wanted to rebel, wanted Dylan. So how did I fix this?

Right now, I knew I couldn't. Just like I couldn't fix what had happened with Trent. My relationship with my brother, or brothers, was now as fractured as my relationship with Dylan. I thought about the kids and their sweet faces, my nieces and nephews. I'd missed them before, when I first stopped being the free family babysitter. Now? I'd never see them again.

Trent was a man of his word. I'd have money deposited into my account, but that would be the only contact I had with the family from now on. But what about my parents? Trent had said Dad had agreed. Did Mom? Surely, not? Mom wouldn't just abandon me like that, would she?

Mom and I had been strangers for a long time. We were nothing alike, and I'd been so caught up in caring for her sons, I guessed I'd never really got to know her. She was just this woman who would show up every now and then, ask for a progress report, and then she'd be off again, to tend to my father and his needs.

Funny how the women in this family served the needs of the men. Even their wives were totally devoted to them. Although, admittedly, all three had, had to fight for their wives. The ladies didn't just lie down and say *okay, fuck me forever.* They'd made a stand. Perhaps that was what I had to do with Trent. I was sure, after a while, he'd see sense. I hoped.

The water started to feel cold, so I got out rather than pour more hot water in. It was time to get out, before I looked like a prune. I couldn't help but check my phone as soon as I went into the bedroom where I'd left it.

Nothing, not even a message from Roxie. Fuck, my life was so empty. I hung my head and pulled the white terrycloth robe tighter around my body. I had nobody to talk to. Wasn't I supposed to have a girlfriend who would bring be me ice cream so we could pig out and watch movies as we ran the man who broke my heart into the ground?

I'd never had a friend like that. Roxie came close, but she was busy. And now? Well, now, I was totally, utterly alone. It was the things that weren't there that hurt the most now. I couldn't go to my sister-in-law, or my friend. I couldn't go to Dylan and ask him to make me forget the pain, the hurt, the anger inside of me. All I could do was sit here, in the dark, and stare at my phone as I'd waited for it to come to life. There had to be someone out there for me. Right?

The really sad part? Even after his ugly words, all I wanted was Dylan's arms to comfort me. But he didn't want me without a contract, and I didn't think I could sign another one. I just didn't think it was in me. With a sigh, I plopped back on the bed and took up staring at the ceiling. What the fuck could I do?

IS MR DARK WORTH ALL THE
TROUBLE?

Would Emily's family really disown her? All her life, she's been 'the Thompson girl', who is she without them?

They say blood is thicker than water, but how often do you come across a man who can fulfil all your darkest desires?

Find out more on
www.amazon.com/dp/B07R2RR9VS

SUMMER COOPER

DISCOVER THE WILD GIRL IN YOU

Besides her love of chocolate, dogs and music... reading and writing is Summer's number one route to escape from crazy friends, family and the in-laws!

She found her own happily ever after with a martial arts fighter who also happens to be an adorable IT geek! Now, she loves to write about hot alpha males that come with a pretty face and covered in tough-as-nails muscle... who are secretly looking for their true soul mate (shhh...)!

Visit her website at
www.summercooper.com

Get in touch at
hello@summercooper.com

CPSIA information can be obtained
at www.ICGtesting.com
Printed in the USA
FSHW010739190519
58265FS